MW01131499

A Yooper's Tale

DEATH BY WENDIGO

Robert Hugh Williams

First Edition

PAGE PUBLISHING
Conneaut Lake, PA

First originally published by Page Publishing 2021

ISBN 978-1-6624-6079-1 (pbk)
ISBN 978-1-6624-6081-4 (hc)
ISBN 978-1-6624-6080-7 (digital)

Printed in the United States of America

Contents

Chapter 1

WENDIGO

Native American lore talks of a terrible cannibalistic creature that devours the flesh of its victims. It's called Wendigo and it is born of the evil deeds of men. This legend of lore stands some fourteen feet tall on two powerful hind legs with yellow glowing eyes that seek its hapless victims in the gloom of darkness. Wendigo, a Cree Indian word, means "evil that devours." Gnashing teeth and large carnivore fangs of the creature rip and consume human flesh with an insatiable appetite. The beast is adorned atop its skull with a crown of antlers, giving it at first the appearance of some great stag on two legs. The

Wendigo is no great deer, however, for those unlucky enough to see one. The beast's face has more the appearance of a huge monster to be part wolf, part demon, and part inexplicable horror. Its appearance exudes pure terror on the beholder and is capable of rendering a victim scared stiff. Its giant muscled body is covered with matted and tangled hair. The creature moves hunched forward as if attacking and dwarfs its victims with its ravenous death-dealing stature. It protrudes claws that are long and sharp, attached to long deadly fingers, in turn attached to muscled arms that appear too long for the body. Its two powerful hind legs have eagle-like feet that seem hairless with talon like claws. Some old legends say that one look from this creature can paralyze the victim with fear and dread as if hit with a neuro toxin. Descriptions of Wendigo vary somewhat among the Algonquian-speaking tribes, but what is true of all the descriptions is that it is a terrible, evil beast that consumes the flesh of men.

The legends and stories of the Wendigo are strongest among the Cree American Indians. The Cree, as one of the Algonquian-speaking nations, are the largest of the Native American tribes and by many are considered to be the First Nation peoples. The term "First Nation people" was bestowed on Indians by Canadians, but here it is meant as the first ancient humans to inhabit North America. The lore of the Wendigo with the Cree peoples echoes through their history with the birth memory of these ancient peoples. Their ancestral home range extends west from James Bay through the Canadian provinces down to the Great Lakes and west of Lake Superior out into North Dakota and the Rocky Mountains.

The accounts of the Wendigo and stories of horror and death have followed the Cree people throughout all their range. Lore of the Wendigo is also traced in many of the related Algonquian-speaking Native American tribes, including the Ojibwa, Chippewa, Huron, Menominee, Noquet, Ottawa, and others in the Great Lakes region. It is no small wonder that the stories of the Wendigo were passed on from generation to generation as more than lore from the old ones. The elders of the local tribes of Minnesota, Northern Wisconsin, and the Upper Peninsula of Michigan would speak of their tribal memories and of accounts with the beast called Wendigo. These hunter-gatherer tribes with ancestral roots of the First Nation peoples believed in this creature of evil. The ancients who first inhabited North America encountered and believed in the Wendigo. The Indian tribes of North America believed in the Wendigo in both its spiritual and physical form.

In modern times, the lore of the Wendigo is still present, but it has become more of a lost dream, like the mammoths that once roamed the lands of the Algonquian-speaking peoples. Tales of modern-day Wendigo encounters seem to be absent in the westernizing tribal cultures. Business council meetings have replaced tribal ceremonies. Economic development, health issues, education, and the basic traditions of language, dance, and heritage have replaced the discussions of lore and lessons of the elders. Times have changed, and the Native American peoples have adapted. Though the First Nation people and modern tribes still hold tight to their connections to Mother Earth, nature, and the life spirit, things have changed. The impact of science, the industrial age, education, and, of course, the Canadian and United States government cannot be denied. New demons like drug and alcohol abuse have replaced Wendigo. New attitudes of society, progress, and modern conveniences of Western civilized culture have become part of the Native American life framework.

With changes of the twentieth and twenty-first century, many passed-down stories are now just lost memories. The Wendigo is now nothing more than the wind talking to the tall white pines in a dark old forest. The lore is now just that, something elders tell the young ones to scare them into good behavior. Yes, the Wendigo is now only a ghost story told around campfires, something not real, something alive only in the imagination…or is it?

Chapter 2

1800S—SILVER JACK DRISCOLL

John Driscoll and his Cree Indian companion Edward Smith were weary of traveling. Their horses plodded along at a steady pace, but it was slow going. They left the lumberjack camps of Saginaw almost over two weeks prior and were finally in Michigan's vast Upper Peninsula rugged wilderness. Springtime was breaking free of winter in Michigan, but here in the rugged terrain of the UP, it was common to get hit with snow well into late spring.

The pair of men was heading into lumber and mining country of the Upper Peninsula to continue prospecting for silver and gold. Driscoll and Smith had been making this annual trek together for almost ten years now. The little explored depths of the Huron and Porcupine Mountains west of Marquette would be their prospecting destinations, but L'Anse would be their stop for this night.

Another hour or so and they would arrive in L'Anse and the soft beds and warm rooms inside the JB Belanger boardinghouse. All the walking and riding was a nice change from working a two-bladed ax and the double-handled saw. Two weeks of traveling by foot, horseback, and barge across the Straits of Mackinac, however, had both men ready for a rest. As John Driscoll thought of the soft bed, he thought to himself that L'Anse would be a fine place to spend the last few days of May and rest up before beginning the prospecting season in the wilds. The horses plotted on, and Driscoll's mind drifted back to the past few days of traveling. The last really good night's sleep had been in Seney a couple nights ago.

Their last overnight had been in a noisy Marquette boardinghouse. Marquette was now becoming a bustling town since its docks had been completed in 1857 and the Soo Locks opening in 1837. There was now a maritime Great Lakes highway opened from the young cities of Chicago and Detroit to what was once the northern UP wilderness town of Marquette. The expanding town had all the commotion for a sleepless night associated with the lumber and mining industry activity that had piled in off the Great Lake steamer *Vienna* from the port of Marquette.

The night before that was a pitched camp on a rocky site overlooking the small community of Munising. The campsite was on a rocky pitch protected from the harsh northern winds but still offered a fantastic view of Lake Superior and Grand Island. Driscoll had heard that Abraham Williams, a fur trader and ironsmith, had managed to purchase most of the island. He was still out there living with his two wives, brood of kids, and a band of Ojibwa Indians who were the original residents of the island. Rumor had it that Cleveland Cliffs Company had approached Williams about selling the island to make into a hunting and vacation area for the mining company executives and their guests.

The night before, Munising was spent at one of the two Seney lumberjack boardinghouses. Seney was a typical Michigan lumber town. There were a couple boardinghouses packed with lumberjack crews, a supply store, a general trading store, a couple liveries, a sawmill, a tannery, and a small population of perhaps fifty or so local residents. There was also a small Catholic missionary, which doubled as a community meeting place. The lumber town was complete with a saloon, which was located at the center of the row of building making up the main street. As was his custom, John Driscoll visited both the Catholic mission house and the saloon to pay his respects.

John had been raised Catholic and still held the belief. He was a lumberjack by trade, though, and a legendary one at that. Being a lumberjack and being a good Catholic weren't exactly complimentary ways of life, but John did his best. Lumberjacks were a tough, hard breed, and John Driscoll was probably the toughest and hardest of them all. He wasn't an ornery or belligerent character. He was a man of few words, and normally they were kindly words, probably because of his Catholic upbringing. If it wasn't for his imposing six-foot-four muscled frame and square chiseled jaw, one might make the mistake of thinking of him only as a gentle giant. He kept his company mostly to Edward Smith and didn't seem to have many other friends, though he did enjoy the company of a woman when one was available. His shock of silver-white hair seemed premature for a man of about forty. His tough, weathered face showed character, strength, and toughness. His eyes were a sea green and mostly kindly, but they could change in an instant and pierce through a man, causing him to dread what was coming next.

The silver hair had come on suddenly about four years before, replacing a thick mane of black hair, almost as if overnight. Few asked about it, though most who knew him wondered what happened. The few that considered themselves friends of John Driscoll, or Jack as he liked to be called, would ask about the hair but only got a menacing scowl or growling retort that he couldn't or maybe didn't want to talk about it. So it was, the man named John Driscoll became known as the legendary lumberjack Silver Jack Driscoll. That was the way Silver Jack Driscoll liked his nickname, Silver Jack...because of his silver hair.

Truth be told, though, there was another reason folks took to calling John Driscoll Silver Jack Driscoll. John Driscoll and his traveling companion Edward Smith tried to keep it a secret, but in a moment of whiskey-induced folly, the secret came out. Not in a blunder of words but in pieces of silver that Edward carried in a deer skin pouch in his coat pocket.

Driscoll and Smith had discovered silver west of Marquette years ago and were mining it during the summer months when the timbering season rested. It was in the same saloon in Seney they were at just a few nights prior, where the silver secret had been revealed three years ago.

On that particular occasion, three years ago, the two were returning from the Huron Mountains and heading back to Saginaw for the winter timbering season. As was Jack's custom, he made the Christian sign of the cross before taking his first shot of whiskey for the evening. A group of Swedish immigrant miners on their way west to the mines of Ishpeming noticed and made a mockery of Driscoll's antics. Unfortunately for young husky Swedes, they didn't know or didn't seem concerned about Driscoll's reputation as a brawler. There were about ten of the young jesters, just the odds that Jack liked in a good brawl. When another half dozen came in from outside, Edward had to jump in and help Jack out. It was then that Edward's coat pocket was torn, and pieces of rough mined silver splashed on the floor. The entire room stopped fighting and just stood and stared. Jack and Edward did what they could to quickly recover the pieces of silver, but a local was quick and had snatched up a couple of the pieces and recognized it a rough mined silver. The cat, in addition to the silver, was out of the bag.

News of the silver spread quickly. In their travels that followed, many asked about the silver, but neither Jack nor Edward would give out any information. It was the following spring while heading back to the Huron Mountains from Saginaw that Jack noticed they were being followed. The two men following them looked to be unsavory characters intent on discovering the location of the silver mine or something worse. The two trailing Jack and Edward were no match in woodcraft and tracking skills. In the end, the two strangers met with an unseemly demise one might call backwoods justice. It became routine that every time Jack and Edward would go into a settlement or town for supplies, they would be followed back into the mountains. As fate would have it, each of the trackers in turn were never seen or heard of again.

By late summer, Jack and Edward were bringing out both silver and gold on their supply runs. Jack and Edward had sole knowledge of the only discovered silver and gold mine in what was now known as iron and copper country. The fact that two common lumberjacks turned part-time prospectors had a couple of secret mines that were producing a fortune in silver and gold was gaining attention. The timber company owners, mining company owners, and other big investors wanted the gold and silver too. Driven by greed, they were offering big rewards for anyone who could find Driscoll's Silver mine or discover other mineable veins of the precious metals. The fact that Silver Jack Driscoll and Edward Smith, a lowly lumberjack and an even lowlier Indian lumberjack, might end up dead didn't matter. All that mattered to these powerful titans of the northern wilderness was getting possession of that fortune of silver and gold.

Jack and Edward did not plan on giving up their secret or ending up dead. The disappearances of trackers trying to discover Jack Silver's mines caused talk and rumors in the settlements and towns throughout the Upper Peninsula and into Wisconsin, Minnesota, and up into Canada. Some thought the trackers died trying to kill Driscoll and Smith. Others thought they just perished in the harsh, rugged Michigan wilderness. And still others thought that the trackers ran across hostile guardians of sacred tribal grounds that resented the White man's encroachment.

Other rumors stirred too. Some of the stories were about curses. Maybe the mines themselves were cursed. Maybe Edward Smith, Cree Indian by birth, was a shaman who could cast a death curse on anyone following them in search of the mines.

There were even wild stories of some terrible beast in the darkness that protected the mines and would kill any trespassers. Some even said the beast was of Indian lore who ate the flesh of men it killed. Yet others said the beast was nothing more than a story being spread by Silver Jack Driscoll and Edward Smith. Maybe even the two men dressed in disguise as a beast to keep the curious novices and ill-intent trackers away.

These rumors and wild stories were usually dismissed as scare tactics to keep trespassers away. Silver Jack Driscoll and Edward Smith were a crafty pair, and many admired their tenacity and creativity to come up with such stories. Yet others were not so sure and thought that maybe there was more truth than fiction in these wild tales.

It was a particular summer four years ago that John Driscoll showed up at one of the Marquette trade and supply stores wearing a crop of silver hair instead of his normal, up until then, head of black hair. Indeed, something strange was going on. The secret location of the gold and silver mines, however, still remained a locked secret known only to Silver Jack Driscoll and Edward Smith.

Even though the UP was its own version of the Wild West, progress was coming. Camps were becoming outposts. Outposts were being developed into towns. Trails were becoming roads, and roads were becoming rail for trains. Immigrants were coming from all over Europe to work the copper and iron ore mines. Lumberjacks, always coming and going, would cut the virgin pines for the different timber operations to bring forth the lumber to build a nation. Cooper from the copper mines in the Upper Peninsula of Michigan would provide over ninety percent of the copper being used to bring America into the industrial age.

The iron ore mined in iron country would be transported by rail and wagon down to Fayette on the Lake Michigan side of the Peninsula. There it would be smelted into pig iron, which in turn would be loaded onto steamer ships and sailed to cities like Chicago and Pittsburg to be made into steel. The steel would be used to build great cities, ships, machines, engines, and automobiles. The metal would serve as the backbone of building America into the Industrial

Age. The land would be tamed, and there was no room for crazy superstitions and fear of the unknown for the companies and wealthy businessmen making fortunes by pillaging vast natural resources of Michigan.

Driscoll's thoughts returned to the present by a quiet whinny from his horse. Darkness was gathering as the two weary figures on horseback, pulling a train of four-pack horses, approached the small logging and mining outpost of L'Anse. Trailing behind, just out of sight, a single rider with a couple of pack horses followed and watched.

Driscoll and Smith checked into the JB Belanger boardinghouse in L'Anse and then put their horses up at the only livery at the outpost. After making sure the horses were well watered and fed, they returned to the small eating hall of the boardinghouse for a hot meal. The meal was venison with gravy, homemade sour dough bread with fresh butter, and sweetened hot coffee to wash it down. In a shadowy corner sat the single rider who had been trailing them, quietly eating his own meal.

Jacob Fiddler was the single rider who now sat inconspicuously in a remote corner of the boardinghouse dining hall. He sat, barely noticed, quietly eating his meal and barely watching Driscoll and Smith scarf down their venison and bread. Jack Fiddler was Cree by birth, average height for a man of the times, muscular build, dark eyes, and black hair cropped close. At first glance, one might not recognize Fiddler as an Indian, but he was. His Cree roots could be traced back to the First Nation peoples. His tribal roots, however, were said to be mixed with the first Whites, large Nordic warriors who came to the lands to the north in great wooden long boats. His face showed the weathered creases of someone carrying fourscore of years as a warrior, explorer, woodsman, and spiritual guide. His eyes were hardened by experiences of near death and sacrifice. Jacob Fiddler had survived fear and evil few men would ever face. Jacob Fiddler was known in his Ontario tribal region as a Wendigo hunter. A shaman of sorts but one of the only known men to have the skill and inner strength to defeat the creature of evil known as Wendigo.

Jacob Fiddler understood the White man, at least he thought he did. He had spent several years living among them and even received a formal education at one of their universities. Fiddler always felt a familiar connection to the Whites but his life flew was always stronger with the tribes.

Driscoll and Smith finally got up from their supper table at the Belanger boardinghouse. Fiddler overheard Driscoll ask for a pint of Dr. Aniston's cure-all medicine from Mr. Belanger, the establishment's owner. The keep was more than happy to fetch a brown bottle topped with a cork and a label that read, "Dr. Aniston's Cure for What Ails You." Driscoll told Mr. Belanger that he felt a bout of grippe coming on and that he and Mr. Smith would be staying a few days until it passed.

That was the last time Jacob Fiddler saw Silver Jack Driscoll alive. Driscoll died two days later in his bed at the Belanger boardinghouse in L'Anse, Michigan. Foul play was not suspected, but for a man with a constitution as strong as Driscoll, to go so quickly just seemed too strange to be a coincidence.

John Driscoll's brother, Saul Driscoll, from Saginaw showed up after about a week and a half later to bury his brother. Fiddler attended the funeral and burial in the Ontonagon cemetery located on the outskirts of L'Anse. There were about forty folks attending the funeral, which was overseen by the Catholic missionary priest from Seney. It seemed that most of the attendees were curious onlookers. Maybe they were just good Christian locals who thought attending the Christian burial was just the right thing to do, one couldn't tell for sure. Edward Smith, Driscoll's faithful traveling companion, was there and served as one of the pallbearers. After the funeral, Edward Smith remained behind and conducted the Cree spirit flight ceremony. The ceremony was for his friend, Silver Jack Driscoll, whose presence and spirit would be missed dearly.

The next day, Jacob Fiddler trailed Edward Smith up to the shores of Lake Superior and then to the trading store in L'Anse. From there, Fiddler trailed Edward Smith deep into the rugged and dark Huron Mountains. First across the Yellow Dog River, then the Dead

River Basin, then into some of the roughest terrain of the Huron Mountains, and finally to the opening of a dark mine shaft.

Edward Smith, the cunning Cree shaman and good friend of Silver Jack Driscoll, was never heard of or seen again. It remains a mystery to this day as to what happened to the mining partner of Silver Jack Driscoll.

As for Jacob Fiddler, he discovered his truth. He would leave the Huron Mountains, stopping only briefly at the L'Anse supply and trade store, then head back to Ontario wilderness to rejoin his tribal clan.

Not once did Jacob Fiddler mention Edward Smith, the mines, or the horrors he encountered in the deep mountains. The hidden location of Silver Jack Driscoll's silver and gold mines somewhere in the Huron Mountains would remain secret. They would be secret to all but perhaps the ghosts of men who died trailing Silver Jack and Edward Smith. Jacob Fiddler was not dead, but the location of Silver Jack Driscoll and Edward Smith's mines would remain a secret that, after many years, Fiddler would take to his grave.

In the wild frontier camps of the UP, it was common talk that dead men could tell no tales. The passing years would turn the stories of gold and silver mines into a UP gold rush. The ambitions of wealth and greed would pass. After some time, the thoughts of Silver Jack Driscoll's gold and silver mines would be but whispers in the tall pines. Silver Jack Driscoll, Edward Smith, silver mines, gold mines would go the way of Paul Bunyan and his blue ox, Babe. They would become nothing but campfire stories and a UP legend.

In nature and in business, it is survival of the fittest. These are just cold hard facts. And so it was with the start-up mining and logging companies in the Upper Peninsula. Many smaller companies were bought out or forced out of business by bigger, stronger, and, in many cases, more ruthless companies. The time period in the Upper Peninsula after Silver Jack Driscoll's death would see this natural culling process with many small start-up companies and more powerful companies pushing or buying them out.

With companies in the UP, investors and money represented strength. Certainly efficient operations, good business practices, and, to a degree, luck would all apply to the formula as to whether a company would survive or not. As the process of natural selection sorted out the survivors, there would come to be a clear divide between the few that owned and invested in the companies and became wealthy and those that applied the muscle, sweat, and blood to make the fortunes for the few. There was definitely a working class and a privileged class developing during the beginnings of the Industrial Age, which was really a nationwide phenomenon. Silver Jack and Edward Smith were part of that working class, but they had managed to keep their fortune and accrue their own wealth. At least, that is, up until the time of Driscoll's death and Smith's disappearance.

As time sorted out the haves and have-nots in the late 1800s and early 1900s, the privileged few, with their power and money, would buy up large tracts of the UP wilderness. Some of the rich and powerful were only interested in making their fortune. Others, however, could see the cost being inflicted on the land. The Upper Peninsula in all its rugged beauty and merciless winters was being scarred by unregulated mining and logging practices.

Some of the most powerful of the elites would purchase vast expanses to preserve the land and the wildlife for their personal and private use. In 1890, a group of these super elites would begin the purchase vast tracts of land in the Huron Mountains and form what was eventually called the Huron Mountain Club (HMC). The Huron Mountain Club, or HMC, was a vast private resort of prime UP wilderness area west of Marquette. There was a limited membership of fifty, exclusively for the elite rich with the purpose of hunting, fishing, hiking, and other recreation. The club would eventually include about thirteen thousand acres, ten thousand of which was old growth virgin timber, several lakes, fifty dwellings, and a huge mansion like log lodge.

Truth be known, however, these rich and powerful moguls of the north were as interested in finding Silver Jack Driscoll's silver and gold mines as they were in having their own private hunting and fishing resorts. The many hired trackers and woodmen, some of the best in the country, were all unsuccessful in discovering the silver and gold mines of Silver Jack Driscoll and his Cree Indian mining partner, Edward Smith. As a result, the giants of the northern mining and timber industry would partner and purchase every tract of land that Driscoll and Smith were rumored to mine. The land of the Huron Mountains was some of the most rugged and beautiful landscape of the Upper Peninsula. That land holding is still private today and is still known as the Huron Mountain Club and still super exclusive. Despite the unlimited resources of these exclusive owners, to date, there has been no discovery of the illusive Driscoll and Edward treasure or mines.

With Driscoll and Smith's cunning ways, is it possible that they fooled even the frontier barons? Is it possible that the mines are so well hidden they still lay undiscovered within the boundaries of the Huron Mountain Club or perhaps even the McCormick Wilderness Area? Is it possible that the mines are not even within the Huron Mountain Club boundaries? Perhaps the mine locations are actually within the confines of what is today the L'Anse Indian Reservation? Perhaps, maybe even, the mine locations are in the depths of the Porcupine Mountains wilderness area?

One thing is for sure: with all the mining exploration in the UP for iron ore, copper, silver, and gold, the Driscoll and Smith mines have never been discovered. It's true that other gold and silver deposits were discovered—much smaller than those in the Western United States—and, in almost all cases, marginally profitable or not profitable at all. The fact remains, however, that Driscoll and Smith's secret mines were never uncovered…at least what was acknowledged publicly.

Chapter 3

WHAT'S A YOOPER? YOUR BRIEF HISTORY LESSON FOR THE DAY

Between the southern shores of Lake Superior (the father of the Great Lakes) and the northern shores of Lake Michigan (the mother of the Great Lakes) lay a paradise. At least that's what Yoopers—the people who live there—will tell you. This land mass called Michigan's Upper Peninsula is connected to the Lower Peninsula of Michigan by a five-mile span of suspension bridge called the Mackinac Bridge. The Mighty Mac (which Michiganders like to call it) was opened for traffic on the first of November 1954, connecting Mackinaw City (southern peninsula) and St. Ignace (Upper Peninsula or UP).

Travel to the UP before the Mighty Mac was by rail barge, ferry, ship, boat, dugout canoe, swimming, or crossing on the hazardous ice during winter. For those who didn't like crossing water, there was always the long way around. Travel down to Chicago up through Wisconsin and then across the UP boarder from the west. Yet again, in modern times, if someone wanted to come down from Canada, they could cross the Sault Ste. Marie International Bridge, finished in 1962, which crosses the St. Marys River (the famous Soo locks) and connects Michigan to Canada on the east side of the Upper Peninsula. Before that, crossing into Canada in Sault Ste. Marie was by barge or a railway bridge.

The people of the Upper Peninsula of Michigan are a kaleidoscope of cultures. Yet, in another sense, they are mixing of subcultures to themselves. To really understand the people of the UP, or as they like to say, Yooper, you really need to take a short trip back in Michigan history.

The Native American Indian tribes are thought to be the first documented human inhabitants of the Upper Peninsula and remain so today. The ancient tribes like the Menominee, Noquet, Ojibwa, and Algonquians maintained a presence in the Great Lakes region for tens of thousands of years. These woodland tribes were all members of Algonquian-speaking peoples. These tribes were all descendants of the First Nation people or the ancients who first inhabited North America. More on that a little later.

The French explorer Étienne Brûlé is said to be one of the first Europeans to explore the Great Lakes region after he arrived in Quebec in 1605. Brûlé and his companions opened the gradual flow of Europeans into the wilderness territory of New France. Brûlé explored, lived among the tribes, and learned their languages, customs, and skills. Brule and his associates facilitated many of the French exploits into the territory. Interestingly, after living many years among the native populations, Brûlé was killed in 1630 and eaten by the Huron Indians whom he had been living with at the time.

French explorers, trappers, and missionaries trekked into the wilderness territory, now called Michigan, in the 1600s and into the mid-1700, as it was considered a French territory. The trappers were in pursuit of furs to sell to European markets. Many of the French stayed on to colonize what would eventually be called the northern Michigan peninsula or Upper Peninsula. Some mingled with the local tribes, some stayed for the fur trade, and some remained to establish French trading posts and colonies. New France was expanding from Quebec westward, through Ontario, and down to the Ohio Valley.

The British came to the new world wilderness to establish their first colony in Jamestown, Virginia, in 1607 and to claim lands for British Empire. British America, as it was called, expanded west from Virginia; north to Newfoundland, conflicting with the French; and south to Florida, conflicting with Spain. Florida at that time was a large tract of land extending from the current-day Florida and up the East Coast to south of Virginia.

Colonial conflicts would erupt between these European powers into what would become known as the Seven Years War in Europe or French and Indian War (1754-1763) in the Americas. Outright hostilities and war on the frontier were triggered by a series of skirmishes between the French and the British. One of those skirmishes occurred when a force of British militia, commanded by then twenty-two-year-old Lieutenant Colonel George Washington, ambushed a French patrol on May 24, 1754, in southwest Pennsylvania. This war would traverse both Europe and the American frontier, including Michigan.

The end result would be British victory and the Paris Treaty of 1763, thus ending the Seven Years War. The treaty would cede Canada and the territory east of the Mississippi River (including Michigan) to Great Britain from the French. Florida would be ceded to Great Britain from Spain, who were allies to the French during the French and Indian War/Seven Years War. The French, in turn, ceded the Louisiana territory to Spain as compensation for Spain's loss of Florida to Britain.

Participants in the French and Indian War on the American frontier included many of Native American tribes. Most of the northern tribes like the Algonquin, Ottawa, Ojibwa, Shawnee, and Wyandot sided with the French. The Cherokee (before 1758), the Iroquois, and the Catawba sided with the British.

Chief Pontiac, an Ottawa chief, did not know of the Paris Treaty of 1763, which formally ended the Seven Years War. He did know, however, that the French had left and the British stayed. Chief Pontiac had great influence with the tribes occupying the frontier lands of Ohio (which included Michigan at that time). On May 7, 1763, Chief Pontiac led a rebellion against the English "dogs clothed in red" by attacking a laying siege to Fort Detroit. During the same period, other tribes attacked British forts and outposts across the region. The intent of Pontiac's rebellion was to drive the British out so the French could return. The siege of Fort Detroit would last for six months and finally end when Pontiac found out about the Treaty of Paris, ending the war, and withdrew. Fort Michilimackinac, located on the southern shores of the straits of Mackinaw, and other forts in the northeast would not fare as well as Fort Detroit.

On June 2, 1763, a Sauk and Ojibwa tribe staged a match of a *baggatiway* (Indian game similar to lacrosse) outside the British occupied fort of Michilimackinac. The fort, strategically located on the southern shores of the Mackinaw straits, had been a trading post built by the French but now was a garrison of British soldiers. British Major George Etherington, charged with command of the fort, was completely fooled by the ruse. The attack was launched and the garrison troops massacred by over two hundred warriors. The whole thing was over before the British could mount a defense. Today a replica of Fort Michilimackinac sits in the exact location as the original French-built fort. Historical actors and reenactments make Fort Michilimackinac a popular tourist attraction.

The Revolutionary War, or the War of American Insurrection as the British folks like to call it, began in 1775 with the battles of Lexington and Concord. That war didn't end so well for the British, and on September 3, 1783, the Paris Treaty of 1783 was signed, formally ending the Revolutionary War.

Many of the American territories gained by Great Britain during French and Indian War, which ended with the signing of the 1763 Paris Treaty, were lost in the 1783 Paris Treaty, ending the Revolutionary War. The Northwest Territory (which Michigan was part of) was ceded to the United States in 1783. The United States, however, did not take control of the Northwest Territory until 1796. At that time, the Northwest Territory included what is now Ohio, Indiana, Illinois, Michigan, Wisconsin, and the northern part of Minnesota.

Great Britain's defeat during the Revolutionary War and the French aligning with the fledgling United States of America meant the fur trade could once again flourish.

With the fur trade prospering, John Jacob Astor, a Waldorf, Germany-born American businessman, established the American Fur Company on Mackinac Island (1808). Astor would become the first multimillionaire in the United States. The War of 1812 (1812–1815), between the British, with their Canadian and Indian allies, and the United States of America, found Astor's fur trade disrupted along the border of Canada and the United States. Astor's American fur company trading posts were seized by British forces. This was a time in Astor's colorful career that he would turn to opium smuggling. In 1816, the American Fur Company purchased ten tons of Turkish opium, which he smuggled to China. In 1817, the US Congress passed a protectionist law that barred all foreign fur traders from the US territories. This, in effect, gave Astor and his American fur company a monopoly on the fur trade around the Great Lakes. With the beginning decline of the fur trade in the 1830s, Astor sold all his holdings in the fur industry and focused on booming real estate market in New York. The American Fur Company on Mackinac Island was only one of many of Astor's entrepreneurial ventures. In retrospect, it could be said that the American Fur Company was a major stepping stone to Astor becoming, in today's standards, the fifth wealthiest man in American history.

Michigan was officially organized as a territory from 1805 to 1837 with Detroit set as its territorial capital. The Michigan Territory initially included what is now the Lower Peninsula and the eastern half of the Upper Peninsula of Michigan.

In 1819, the Michigan territory was expanded to include all of the Upper Peninsula, Wisconsin, and part of Minnesota. As Michigan was pushing for statehood, a property dispute erupted, resulting in a "bloodless" Toledo War or Michigan-Ohio War (1835–1836).

The disputed land was known as the Ohio strip, which both states claimed. Michigan's twenty-four-year-old "boy governor," Steven T. Mason, was unwilling to cede the Ohio strip. Michigan would finally concede in December 1836 during what was called the Frostbitten Convention. Governor Mason only finally agreed to a resolution with pressure from the US congress and President Andrew Jackson himself. The compromise, Michigan finally reluctantly accepted, was the Upper Peninsula in exchange for the Ohio strip. At the time, Michigan felt it had received a raw deal, but at least it opened the door for statehood. Unknown to Governor Mason and the Michigan congress, a rich reserve of copper, iron ore, and forest in the UP would, in fact, resolve the dire financial situation Michigan was in at the time.

On January 26, 1837, Michigan, with the UP included, was officially recognized as the twenty-sixth state of the union of the United States. In the 1840s, American prospectors began arriving in the UP in search of copper, and thus began the Michigan copper rush.

At that time, pieces of copper could be found in streams or even on the ground. During the time period 1850 to 1881, the copper mines of Michigan's Upper Peninsula would produce three quarters of all copper produced in the United States. In 1869, more than 95 percent of all copper produced in the US came from Michigan's Upper Peninsula.

Michigan's copper was well known before the copper rush of the 1840s. There is evidence that the natives of North America mined the copper of the UP as far back as 5000 BC, working the metal to make tools, weapons, and trading. In the 1700s, members of the Ojibway showed early French explorers and missionaries the copper laden throughout the UP's copper country, including the Ontonagon Boulder. The Ontonagon Boulder is probably the most famous piece of UP native copper (though not the biggest) to be removed from the Ontonagon River in 1843. It was once a sacred stone of the UP tribes, and today one could visit the 3,708 pounds of UP native copper in the Department of Mineral Sciences, National Museum of Natural History, at the Smithsonian Institute. If visiting the UP, though, a replica of the boulder can be viewed in the Ontonagon historical museum. The history of the Ontonagon Boulder is a fascinating one—from a sacred Native American boulder to the sale to Whites, the jostling of ownership, extracting and moving the huge piece of copper, ownership by the Department of War, and finally the Smithsonian Institute. Even in recent history (1991), the Keweenaw Bay Community tried, unsuccessfully, to repatriate the Ontonagon Boulder as a sacred Indian relic.

From the mid-1800s and well into the mid-1900s, the Upper Peninsula would be hurdled, and sometimes dragged, into the America's industrial age. The lucrative fur trade would meld into the age of iron ore mines, copper mines, and timbering. Many fortunes would be made by the exploitation of Michigan and her Upper Peninsula's natural resources. A steady of flow of European immigration would provide the sweat equity for these major exploits. Swedes, Finns, Germans, Cornish, early English, and early French-Canadian settlers would migrate into the UP for work and the promise of a better life.

It was also during this century, mid-1800 through mid-1900, that an emerging nation would realize that seemingly endless resources would, in fact, have an end. Wildlife populations would decline with unregulated hunting. The landscape was left scarred by timber barons, who, after cutting their fortune from the virgin timber, would abandon the land without replanting. The mining companies would develop mines, some open pit, some slant mine shafts, some deep vertical shafts thousands of feet deep to get down to the strata veins of the iron ore or copper. Little was known, understood, or cared about in terms of toxic byproducts of mining operations. The goal of these commercial operations was to extract the resource as quickly and cheaply as possible. After all, there was a nation to build, wars to fight, and fortunes to be made.

In nature and in business, it is survival of the fittest. These are just cold hard facts. Man is of nature, and basic universal natural laws are what they are—not good, not bad, just... "they are what they are." And so it was with the start-up mining and logging companies in the Upper Peninsula. Many smaller companies were bought out or forced out of business by bigger, stronger, and, in many cases, more ruthless companies. This time period in the Upper Peninsula would see this natural culling process with small start-up companies. With companies in the UP, investors and money represented strength and power. Certainly efficient operations, good business practices, and, to a degree, luck would all apply to the formula as to whether a company would survive or not. As the process of natural selection sorted itself out, there would come to be a clear divide between the few that owned and invested in the companies and became wealthy and those that applied the muscle, sweat, and blood to make the fortunes for the few. There was definitely a working class and a privileged class developing during the beginnings of the industrial age, which was really a nationwide phenomenon. As time sorted out the haves and have-nots, the privileged few, with their power and money, would buy up large tracts of the UP wilderness. As time passed, the nation, along with Michigan, would adapt and evolve.

To some folks, the Upper Peninsula might be a lakeshore paradise vacation between the last two weeks of July and the end of the second week of September. To others, it might be paradise in October and November when the fall colors come into their prime and all the events of fall harvest take place like hunting, fishing, and festivals. Yet to others, their visit to paradise comes in the middle of winter as the caravans of pickup trucks and trailers loaded with snowmobiles, skis, snow shoes, or maybe dogs and dogsleds trek north across the Mighty Mack to enjoy all the winter that the Michigan's Upper Peninsula has to offer.

In any event, Michigan's Upper Peninsula, with its diverse and unique cultural history, endless outdoor wonders and activities, rustic wilderness areas, great lakeshore lines, rivers and lakes, and unique location, is a place worth visiting, enjoying, and living.

Chapter 4

DEATH BY SUICIDE

Her long black hair lay strung across her face, almost covering the noose clenched tight around her neck. She must have been pretty... no...beautiful when her skin was flush with life. But now, as the Marquette and Northern Michigan University Campus police cordoned off the small white house with black trim, her eyes bulged out in a very unflattering and sickening way. Death was not pleasant to look at, even after the mortician would do his best to doctor things up and make her pretty again.

A small crowd of students, some going to class, some returning, began to gather on the sidewalk and street in front of the house. It was about two o'clock on a Thursday afternoon. This Marquette neighborhood was typical of a "campus rental" neighborhood with lots of smaller houses to rent to students who were either attending college or working or both. Most of the houses were block, ranch, or Cape Cod style. Some of the older homes were two-story, reminiscent of the mining and logging times in this area a century ago. The dwellings were close together and, for the most part, well maintained, except in some cases where tributes to last night's party littered the yard. There was nothing unusual about this house. It was a Cape Cod, painted white, with black trim, a long driveway, and small fenced backyard. Three female students were renting it. Two of the women were from down state, and the third, the one dangling in the hangman's noose, was from the Upper Peninsula... L'Anse, to be exact.

While the cops were doing their thing, investigators were looking around, taking pictures, dusting for and lifting fingerprints, and questioning neighbors. Student suicides were not uncommon, but the timing of this one didn't make sense and didn't fit any of the normal profiles. Typically, student suicides occurred during periods of high stress…exams, relationship breakups, moving, financial problems, or family problems or some combination of all. Nadia Red Horse, the deceased, was a second-year sophomore on full academic scholarship. Her grades were good—very good, in fact—finances bearable, and she had lots of friends and was a likable, popular student on campus. Her home life seemed good with hardworking parents, who were still together, and several brothers and sisters. The fact that she would commit suicide in the middle of the first semester, with everything going for her, just didn't fit.

Detective Stannis Ryker of the Marquette city police department was assigned the case. Ryker, nicknamed Stan, was a blond-haired Swede, six feet and three inches, with the build of a linebacker; he was forty-two years old. His father and grandfather had worked the iron mines of Michigan's Upper Peninsula. Stan Ryker, with his close-cut crop of blond hair, had played college football right here at Northern Michigan University, in Marquette. He joined the Marines right out of high school but, after his four-year hitch, came back home to Marquette, started college, and made the football team as a walk-on. Though he was the offspring of miners, he chose a different path—law enforcement. He loved being a cop and he loved being in his hometown, protecting the people he grew up to know. Aside from his excessive gambling habit, Detective Ryker was an upstanding member of the community. On all appearances, Ryker was a good cop, well liked and well respected by the locals.

It looked like suicide, all right, including the handwritten suicide note, but Ryker's instincts didn't settle easy on this first impression. Something was off, and it was more than just the timing of the death. Everything in the house and outside was in place where it was supposed to be. No signs of robbery, nothing unusual or out of place. Actually, everything was almost too neat and orderly for being the house of college kids. Being a good detective, though, Stan

Ryker would stuff his gut instincts in his pocket for now and let the evidence, forensic investigation, and autopsy lead to whatever they would find.

The investigations, interviews, notifications, site cleanup, and autopsy all proceeded and ended quickly. The coroner ruled the death a suicide. There was no extra hoopla or mysterious circumstances. That was it...suicide...suicide, plain and simple...case closed. Detective Ryker didn't like it, but there it was...plain as day...with nothing substantial to prove otherwise.

The normal student candlelight vigils would take place for Nadia Red Horse. There would be solemn moments of silence in classrooms. The local churches and chapels would offer up prayers for the family and friends. Grief and trauma counseling would be offered for students who needed it. The tribe would hold their burial ceremony and pass her soul on to the next world.

In the end, Nadia Red Horse would still be dead...a life ended without reason. Then, after a brief period of mourning, campus life would go on as if nothing happened. The only memory of Nadia Red Horse would be a plaque of remembrance on the student center wall, a cold headstone, and an empty void in the hearts of her family and friends.

While the yellow police tape was being taken down from the white Cape Cod house with black trim, the word of the suicide was spreading like wildfire across campus. The suicide would hit the local news channels that evening. Campus officials would publicly announce their invigorated plan for campus suicide prevention. Life would move on in Marquette, Michigan. All the key players would take the steps and say the right things to make sure life moved on. The university president, the police chief, and all the talking heads on the local news would try to bring closure to the suicide. It would all push forward like the predictable ticking of a clock.

Chapter 5

VOID

At the main campus cafeteria, a small group of friends gathered for an evening meal before hitting the books that night. There was a void, however, and it was as noticeable as the vacant chair and the collective hollow of the heart of this tight-knit gathering of friends. That void could have been a loud scream or the dead silence of nothingness…or maybe both in one agonizing gasp.

The news of Nadia Red Horse's death had hit them collectively, like a punch to the gut. She… Nadia…had an empty place at their table. A place for her…she was supposed to be there now… with them. It just didn't make any sense. Why would Nadia commit suicide? Why now? She was their close friend and she gave no indications of depression, troubles, or suicide. In fact, it was just the opposite. She was excited about life. She was optimistic about classes, her grades, her family coming to visit her at campus, and even her new boyfriend. It simply didn't make one iota of sense.

No one spoke for a long time. Everyone just sat picking at their trays of food, as if pretending to eat. Finally, Caden Garrett broke the silence. His words were steady and reassuring. There was no easing the shock or waking everyone up from a bad dream. Caden had known death before. In Afghanistan and Iraq, he had seen friends killed. He had seen it close up. He had physical scars from wounds and occasional nightmares to remind him. No, death sucked. It sucked even more when it was a good friend. Nadia's suicide, though, put a new twist to death that he wasn't used to. In Caden's mind, he knew he should have seen it coming, something, or anything that told him something was wrong. The whole group felt the guilt of not seeing something, anything, to prevent Nadia's seemingly senseless suicide.

Caden Garrett stood six feet one, brown hair cut short…military style, face covered in a full well-trimmed beard. He was lean and muscular, and when he moved, it was like a lion, easy and relaxed but sure and with purpose. He was kind, funny, and playful with his friends. In a fight or tight spot, however, he was the guy you wanted on your side. His eyes could turn to piercing intensity, and his entire body could become a weapon of bone-breaking destruction. Caden didn't advertise his skills in martial arts or his combat skills, but he worked out regularly at a local dojo and with a local mixed martial arts gym to stay in shape and maintain his edge. His time as an Army Ranger and later as an operator with Task Force Green gave him his "PhD" in life experience. At the age of twenty-six, he had seen more death and destruction than most would ever see in a lifetime. One never knows when the combat and survival skills would be needed. Always better to be ready than not.

Nina Orend was sitting next to Caden and watched as he talked. Watching more than listening, really. Her eyes were still red from tears and the pain of Nadia's death. The shock of Nadia's suicide had hit Nina hardest of all. More accurately, Nina was still in shock. She had run to her cousin's house when she heard the news on campus and got there just in time to see the EMTs haul Nadia's body out of the house. The sight nearly crushed her right then and there.

Nina Orend was Caden Garrett's girlfriend and Nadia Red Horse's cousin. Nina and Nadia had been close, both growing up together in L'Anse. Nina was a beauty just like Nadia. In high school, they were nicknamed the "heartbreak" twins even though they were only cousins. They were both tomboy types preferring hunting, fishing, camping, and sports to prom dresses, shopping, and girly gossip. Nina was tough, but losing Nadia felt unbearable. Having Caden there helped.

Across the table sat Mingan Grey Wolf and Callie Catrin. Mingan Grey Wolf had served with Caden in the Ranger Regiment and again with Delta. Life experiences in the military had made them best friends. Callie Catrin was Caden Garrett's younger cousin from down in Schoolcraft County of the Upper Peninsula. Callie's father was Caden's uncle on his mother's side.

Mingan and Caden were best friends and considered themselves blood brothers. Not through tribal tradition per se but through the forges of combat, blood, sweat, and near-death experiences. Brothers in combat would forge bonds as tight as any tribal blood brothers. Many missions together in Afghanistan and Iraq would do that…if you survived.

Mingan Grey Wolf, or Mingo as Caden nicknamed him, stood five feet and ten inches tall. Shorter than Caden Garrett, Mingan was powerfully built and a natural athlete. He had declined playing college football over focusing on an education. It was a decision his parents and he himself had questioned many times since. Mingan, in contrast to Caden, chose to grow his hair out after the military. Mingan Grey Wolf with his black shoulder-length hair, chiseled face, and dark brown eyes could cast either a friendly, inviting smile or the fearsome look of a man hard as steel. Both Mingo and Caden had soft friendly demeanors, but each in their own right could be a force to be reckoned with.

Callie Catrin liked hanging out with her big cousin Caden and his friends. Callie, or Kat as her friends nicknamed her, was a blonde spitfire with her five-foot-four stature and mischievous blue eyes. She quickly became part of their tight-knit group. Caden introduced her to the group back during freshman orientation in August before she started her freshman classes. Caden treated Callie as his little sister, and so did the others…not his little sister per se but *their* little sister. Kat was smart, quick-witted, and had a warm personality that could bring a smile to the most depressed person. Callie was the group's favorite "little sister," and that was how she was treated…special and spoiled.

Troy Jackson and Sydney Willington rounded out the group. Troy Jackson was from downstate and your classic bookworm…kind of. He had an IQ that was said to be off the charts and could bore anyone to death with details of just about any subject. To his credit, he was also a prankster and comedian, at least within the confines of their group. Sydney Willington, or Syd as she was nicknamed, was the studious type with plain brown hair and a shy personality. Troy and Sydney seemed to bring out the best in each other. They weren't a couple, but they seemed to be best friends. The rest of the group often wondered why they weren't dating each other…or thought they were or were and just not telling anyone.

After about an hour of small talk and picking at food grown cold, it was decided that they would head out to get a few hours of studying. The group would meet up again later, about 11:00 p.m. at a local pub to have a few drinks and ponder the suicide mystery some more. More questions would be discussed, but it wouldn't change anything except surface more questions. There was a lot to think about and discuss, like Nadia's funeral, meeting with her family, and helping any way they could. It was only Thursday, so they would have the weekend to try to start to sort through the grieving process.

Yes, death by suicide sucked…big-time.

Chapter 6

PRIVILEGED FEW

Dirk Astor yelled at the man in the guard shack to open the fucking gate. The man in the gatehouse had been dozing off. The security guard scowled at the silver Mercedes Rover with tinted windows until it pulled up and stopped. When he saw the driver was Dirk Astor, the guard turned red with embarrassment and instantly broke out in a sweat. Dirk Astor called him a lowlife, local yokel, piece of shit, and he threw a hot cigarette butt at him and then drove on into the paved roads of the Huron Mountain Club grounds. As the Rover spun out, kicking gravel and stone all over the guardhouse, Tom Martin, the security guard, could hear Dirk Astor's friends howling with laughter in the back seat.

It was Friday midafternoon, and Dirk Astor, with his buddies from Michigan Technological University in Houghton, was spending the weekend at the Astor lodge within the Huron Mountain Club. The long weekend break from Michigan Tech was a welcomed break. Studies were such a pain in the ass.

The Astor lodge had been in the Astor family shortly after the founding of the Huron Mountain Club in the late 1800s. In fact, the Astor family was one of the first of a super-rich and elite group of owners to found the exclusive Huron Mountain Club. As founding members, they would ensure that the membership remained exclusive and secretive.

Dirk Astor's great-grandfather (five times removed), John Jacob Astor, was the original owner of part of the property lands where the founding of the Huron Mountain Club would begin. John Jacob Astor began amassing his fortunes with the American Fur Company on Mackinac Island in the early 1800s. John Jacob Astor would continue building his fortune through the opium trade between China and Turkey when the war of 1812 disrupted fur revenues. Finally, John Jacob Astor would take his fortunes to New York and continue growing his financial empire in real estate.

Even after moving to New York, the elder John Jacob Astor treasured this great wilderness of the North and staked part of his legacy in a large tract of land northwest of the budding harbor town of Marquette at that time. In the 1890s, John Jacob Astor's eldest son, John Theodore Astor, along with Cyrus McCormick and Frederick Miller, would purchase the initial tract of the twenty-four thousand acres that would become known as the exclusive and secretive Huron Mountain Club. The club was so exclusive that even Henry Ford was put on a waiting list when he applied for membership. To the inner circle of owners at the time, the property was mining investment rather than the private exclusive hunting property as purported to the public.

So it was that young Dirk Astor was born with a silver spoon well implanted in his mouth and part of "American royalty" of the rich. His father, grandfather, and great-grandfathers had managed to hold or improve on the family fortune and establish business and family roots throughout North America and be known in many circles as old money. This old money would be part of the building blocks for many of the Astor holdings and investments. Financial investments that had tentacles into many of the corporations during America's booming Industrial Revolution beginning around 1850. It was a time when the United States was becoming a superpower and the Astors were part of that legacy. As times ushered into the twenty-first century, the Astors diversified into the computer age to maintain and continue growing the family fortunes.

Yes, Dirk Astor was bred and born of privilege and money. His family legacy was undisputable and undisputed. With this legacy of "American royalty," extravagant wealth, and privilege, Dirk Astor carried an arrogant chip on his shoulder of superiority and smugness that would breed the contempt of lesser people.

The young Astor was an only child and spoiled rotten while growing up. Now, at the age of twenty-three, his privilege was still unhampered, but he was no fool. He had always been a good-looking kid while growing up in New York under the tutelage of his father and mother, Jack and Judith Astor. Jack and Judith Astor were well known as one of America's power couples. They were each political animals in their own right with influence in Washington, business and politics. They both knew how to throw their political weight around and did it without hesitation. Either you rule people or you get ruled. That was one of the cornerstones of having and keeping power. It was a family tenant passed down from one generation to the next. Dirk Astor learned the rules early while growing up in the world of New York politics. He was smart, handsome, and charismatic when he wanted to be. Dirk Astor was a privileged young man and a quick study to the ways of politics, power, and wealth.

The young Astor seemed to be born for the art of politics. He used manipulation, deceit, and anything at his disposal to get what he wanted, no matter what the cost to other people. Yes, Dirk Astor was ruthless. He was as a kid growing up and still was as a young man going to college. It was sport for Dirk Astor to throw his power, money, and influence around. He did it because he could and because it was good entertainment—for him and his friends.

On the other hand, Dirk Astor could also be a real charmer and ladies' man when he wanted. He could turn on his GQ good looks and boyish charm in a heartbeat. Many a good girl was turned bad before she knew what was happening while in the company of Dirk Astor. Of course, a little gamma h or liquid ecstasy always helped—that is, if the cocaine, weed, or alcohol didn't do the trick.

So the game for this weekend would be making sport with the local ladies and enjoying the exclusive surroundings of the club, as Dirk liked to call the Huron Mountain Club. Dirk Astor and his pack of silver-spoon buddies would descend on Marquette this Friday night, pick up some of the local girls, and bring them back to the Huron Mountain Club. While at the Astor Lodge and beautiful surroundings of the club, Dirk and his pack of friends would feast on their innocence. There was nothing quite like fresh new pussy to spice up the weekend for Dirk Astor and his friends. After all, these locals were here for their sport and entertainment.

Chapter 7

CIRCLE OF LIFE...AND DEATH

The weekend passed quickly for Caden Garrett and Nina Orden. Studies, talking to Nadia's parents, and making arrangements to get Nadia's body to L'Anse for the funeral consumed most of their time.

This was the end of September in the Upper Peninsula, and the leaves of the trees were turning with their brilliant cloaks of color. Fall was Caden's favorite time of the year. The changing season, the fall colors, and, of course, the beginning of hunting season—this is what autumn was all about for Caden Garrett. Six years in the military, six combat tours, and now the vigor of college studies put a damper on his time for hunting. No matter...sometimes it was just thinking about it that made everything good. Now, with fall colors on campus, time with Nina, and the turning of the season, everything was still good except for the fact, of course, that one of their best friends had recently died.

Nadia's funeral took place that Wednesday in L'Anse. It was mostly a family and tribal affair, but some NMU students and one administrator, about fifteen total, came to pay respects to Nadia's family. Many in the tribe took Nadia's suicide particularly hard. Especially, Nadia's high school friends and teachers. Nadia had been a standout student, an athlete, and the "reluctant" homecoming queen. She was a promising star to the small community of L'Anse and destined, in the minds of many, for great and wonderful things—that is, until this happened.

Caden, Nina, Mingo, Kat, Troy, and Syd stayed at the small community center to help clean up after the reception following the graveside funeral service. As funerals go, it was perfect. The service was held outside and surrounded by the brilliant fall colors. Traditional graveside burial words were spoken by the town reverend. Additionally, an Indian burial ceremony was performed by a local tribe member to give Nadia a proper send-off into the next life. True, it was sad, painful, and tearful, but as the circle of life goes, this funeral did what was intended. It brought closure to Nadia's death and provided the appropriate step in the grieving process.

The one thing the funeral service did not do, however, was answer the question why. As family and friends gathered afterward at the local community center, the question why only seemed to get louder and asked more often. Why did Nadia commit suicide? Why by hanging? And where was Nadia's new boyfriend…the one she was so excited about? He didn't come to the service; in fact, no one had seen or heard of him since before the discovery of Nadia's lifeless body.

Accepting the reality of Nadia's death was finally being grasped in the minds of family and friends. These were the people who were initially unbelieving when getting hit by the cold shock of the news of her death. Accepting her death and understanding it, however, were two different things. With Indian culture, and human existence for that matter, the circle of life and death were understood and accepted. Nadia's death could be accepted. The reason why, however, was yet to be understood.

The drive back to Marquette was uneventful until the town of Michigamme. Mr. Bookworm, Troy Jackson, almost shit himself when the beast crossed in front of his van and he jammed on the breaks. A young bull moose crossed the road in front them after passing through the small town of Michigamme. Troy's van, an old Dodge Caravan, almost slammed into the young bull as they coursed toward the outskirts of town headed toward Marquette. The young Bull Moose strolled across the road in front of them, as if he owned the road. An animal that size *could* own the road unless the driver was behind the wheel of a cement truck or 18-wheeler. Troy Jackson was not behind the wheel of a cement truck…only his old beat-up van.

Seeing the moose seemed to bring the group of friends back to life. Riding together in Troy's van had been the smart thing to do. It didn't look like much, but it was reliable. All six of them could fit, and it would save on the gas money. Students didn't usually have a lot of extra spending cash, so they were always looking for ways to save for important things like food…and beer. The moment the moose stepped in front of them, everyone forgot about the sadness of Nadia's death and gazed in amazement as the large brown beast stood there, then casually walked off into the trees.

Moose were native to Michigan's Upper and Lower Peninsula but had been wiped out during the 1800s because of overhunting and lack of hunting regulations. Any wild game was food, and there was requirement for wild game to feed a growing population. Moose had been reintroduced to the Upper Peninsula in the 1930s, but the effort was largely unsuccessful. Most of the moose were poached or succumbed to brain worm. Again, moose were reintroduced in the 1980s, and a breeding population still roams the UP today. In previous centuries, prior to European settlement, the native tribes could hunt a vibrant population of moose. These days, however, the moose population hasn't yet achieved huntable numbers like the days of the first peoples. So, in many ways, it was a special treat for the group to see this bull moose.

Almost as suddenly as the animal appeared on the road in front of them, it vanished into the thick brush. With this moose sighting, the group began seeing life in a different lens. Maybe the moose had woken them from their grieving dream state. The fact that fall colors were coming into their prime and the fact that it was fall in the Upper Peninsula suddenly dawned on them. Fall had been Nadia's favorite time of year. She would be happy now. Excited, actually, though she was always optimistic. It was as if this moose was a sign, a sign from Nadia, that she would want them to move on. Yes, it felt like Nadia would want them to move on and be happy. Nadia was there in spirit, and she would push them forward where they needed to go.

As if on cue, the conversation ticked up and became livelier now. Finally, there was an air of optimism in the van…definitely more positive, and everyone felt it. Troy was joking how he had just missed his opportunity to cash out his van if he had hit the moose. Cat rolled her eyes and said she didn't feel much like walking if he had hit the moose. Looking at Sydney, Cat said, "I think you need to take him out to have his head examined." Troy and Syd both laughed. Mingo glanced at Caden and Nina, smiled, and said, "I do believe it was her spirit." Caden nodded back, smiled and pulled Nina closer, and kissed her on the forehead. Nina's brown eyes, still red from tears, looked up at Caden. Nina snuggled in closer and enjoyed the feeling of being close to the guy she loved.

The group of friends would go on without Nadia. She would be remembered and she would be kept in their hearts. When they got back to Marquette, they would begin the "student shuffle" again—attending classes, meeting for the evening meal, and doing the best they could. None of them came from well-to-do families, so they kept their noses to the grind and kept working toward the piece of paper that they would get at the end of their student struggles. And thus, the circle of life and death would continue.

Chapter 8

MISSING STUDENT

A week had passed since Nadia's funeral. Campus life was a bustle for Caden. First class, 8:00 a.m. Second class, 10:00 a.m. Third class, 2:00 p.m. That was Monday, Wednesday, and Friday. Usually he would meet up with Mingan Grey Wolf, his best friend Mingo, for lunch on Monday, Wednesday, and Friday. On Tuesdays and Thursdays, he would meet up with Nina for lunch. Tuesdays and Thursdays were his "two class" days. First class at 10:00 a.m. and then another at 2:00 p.m. There were the class schedules, meeting for lunch, workout times, study times, meet for supper, more study time. It was busy.

Caden and Mingo were rooming together in a two-bedroom apartment. His cousin Callie Catrin, or Kat, shared an apartment with Nina in the same apartment complex. Kat was able to get an exception to campus policy and take an apartment instead of the mandatory freshman dorms because of no vacancies. The exception was conditional with Kat's parents' signatures and based on her grades.

Mr. and Mrs. Catrin, Kat's parents, were willing to sign off on the exception to dorm condition only because Kat had an apartment lined up in the same building as their nephew Caden. Jake and Susan Catrin trusted their nephew Caden and looked to him as a son. Caden's parents had been killed in a car crash when he was fourteen years old. The Catrins took him in and treated him as the son they never had. For Kat, it was wonderful. She always liked Caden and looked up to him as a big brother even though they were only cousins. Caden was always grateful to his uncle Jake and aunt Susan for taking him in.

Moving from a big high school downstate to a smaller "Yooper" high school had gone better than expected. It was the middle of his freshman year in high school. His parents' death in a car accident had hit him hard. As it was, his aunt Susan was able to come down and assist with settling his parents' affairs, get a lawyer, and do the proceedings to take legal guardianship of Caden. It all seemed to happen quickly, and Caden was a Yooper transplant in no time at all. The locals in Manistique were friendly and accepting. The fact that he was a good kid and contributed his talents to their sports teams also helped.

The transition to the military after graduating high school happened quickly. Caden had an offer to play football at Ferris State University in Big Rapids, Michigan, and another offer to wrestle at Grand Valley State University, near Grand Rapids, but neither appealed to him at this point in his life. He wanted something different. His uncle Jake had retired from the military and had been an airborne ranger, Special Forces, and with Delta Force. That was more the line of thinking for Caden—military first, then college.

Caden had been daydreaming as he ate. Nina laughed at him when she had asked a question, and he didn't even hear it. Today was Tuesday, "lunch with Nina" day...only two classes today. It seemed that she was always happy to see him. Caden liked that. He was always happy to see her but maybe didn't express it well enough. He could be a little broody at times, especially when his thoughts were focused on school, class, a project, or hunting. That's just the way he was.

Caden's cell phone rang... Uncle Jake. Nina watched as Caden nodded, gave a couple short yes and no replies, and finally said, "Let me see how my schedule shapes up. I will give you a call Thursday and let you know for sure." Nina had seen the phone light up with Jake Catrin's name when it rang. "Hot date for this weekend?" she asked.

"Yep," Caden winked back, "and you are invited." Nina laughed. Caden went on to tell Nina about Uncle Jack's invitation to come down to Schoolcraft County this coming weekend for some archery deer hunting and maybe some grouse hunting. "He also said that I would have to bring Kat with me, and I could bring you if you behave."

That got Nina laughing. "Me? What about you! And as far as that goes, what about Kat! You two are the troublemakers!" Both Caden and Nina laughed. They kissed…then they each took off in a separate direction for class.

It was 10:00 p.m., and Nina was back in her apartment room with Kat. Nina had just got back from her study group and was settling in. Kat was on her cell phone texting some guy she had met in one of her classes. Nina's cell chimed…it was Caden. "Hey, babe! Your place or mine…or pass?"

Nina smiled, and Caden could feel it over the phone. "Whose bed did we mess up last?"

Caden could feel his heart jump and laughed out loud. "Well, I have clean sheets on my bed, so I guess it's mine!"

Nina was happy and almost giggled. "Be over in fifteen minutes…just want to talk to Kat for a minute first."

Caden sat in the recliner looking at the TV while he waited for Nina. It was the local news. The talking head was saying something about a local NMU student being missing, and local authorities were asking for the public's assistance if they knew of the whereabouts of this student. Again, the talking head gave a brief description of the missing guy, then flashed a picture on the screen. Caden hadn't really been watching closely until he saw the face. "Holy shit!" The picture, and now Detective Stannis Ryker of the Marquette police department, with a split screen on the TV, was asking for the public's help in locating this male student. On the TV was Detective Ryker talking on one side of the split screen. On the other side was a picture of the missing student, Erik Thompson… Nadia's new boyfriend.

Five minutes later, there was a knock on the apartment door. Caden got up, looked through the peephole, and saw it was Nina. He opened the door to her beaming smile and a big kiss. "Come on in, hot stuff," Caden whispered as he grabbed her around the waist and firmly on one buttock cheek, briefly biting and sucking playfully on her neck. Nina's eyes widened and then narrowed with hot intent as she perked her lips around his earlobe and gave it a tongue-filled suck. "You are in trouble now, buddy!" She giggled, closed and locked the door, and took his hand to pull him into the bedroom. Caden followed, thinking to himself, *God, I love this crazy woman!*

The alarm went off way too early. Caden looked around and smiled. His bed was messed up. The woman he loved, lying there in a tangle of sheets, blankets, and pillows. He smiled again and gave Nina a bite-filled kiss on her firm butt cheek. She opened her eyes, smiling while she looked at Caden, and pulled him close to wrap herself around him in a tight hug. "I'm never going to let you go," she told him.

"You better not," Caden replied. "But for right now, I have to get to my eight-o'clock class. Test today." Nina smiled, kissed him, and told him she would be heading out for class too shortly...but after coffee. "We will talk at supper. I saw something important on the news last night," Caden called just before closing the door and heading out for class.

Nina was half done with her cup of coffee when her phone rang. She didn't recognize the number, but it was a local number. "Hello," she answered.

"Is this Nina Orend?" came the male voice on the other end of the call.

"Yes," Nina replied, still not recalling the owner of the voice.

"This is Detective Stannis Ryker with the Marquette police department. Do you have a moment to talk?"

Nina was surprised but told the detective yes. Ryker asked if he could meet her somewhere to ask her some questions. Nina hadn't seen the news last night, and Caden hadn't mentioned anything, so she had no idea why this detective would want to talk to her. "Sure, meet me at the NMU campus main cafeteria at 6:00 p.m. I'll be with my friends."

Ryker clarified which cafeteria it was and then said, "Okay, as a matter of fact, I would like to talk to them too."

Nina hung up, feeling puzzled and confused. She then sent a text to Caden to let him know they would have an extra "companion" sitting with them at supper.

Ryker was sitting and waiting for them as each of the group members showed up. Ryker almost looked like he could be a member of the NMU student body or maybe a part of the staff with his casual jeans, flannel shirt, and NMU letter jacket. Ryker eyed each student with a scrupulous but friendly eye as they approached the table and set their food trays down. Detective Ryker introduced himself in a friendly but professional way as each person came to the table—first Caden, then Nina, Kat, Mingo, Troy, and finally Syd, who came to join the group five minutes late.

Ryker sized up the group and each individual as he watched them approach, shake his hand, and then take a seat. It was a bit of an odd group with the two jock types, Caden Garrett and Mingan Gray Wolf, and the bookworm types, Troy Jackson and Sydney Willington. And then there was Nina Orend, who made a striking resemblance to Nadia Red Horse…the suicide girl. And then there was the short attractive blonde with the friendly smile and beaming blue eyes.

Everyone started eating the cafeteria food on the trays in front of them while watching and listening to Detective Ryker. He started by mentioning the local news report last night and the missing college student, Erik Thompson. He also said he knew that Thompson had been dating Nadia Red Horse, the suicide girl, looking specifically at Nina to watch her expression. Nina saw it and stated that Nadia was her cousin but that they grew up more like sisters and were very close. Caden spoke up and told Ryker that they were all friends with Nadia and that she was a part of this group of friends. Ryker offered his condolences to the group, specifically Nina.

Detective Stan Ryker had a way of working with students that set them at ease and made them feel comfortable and not threatened. He took a sip of his coffee and took a bite of his apple pie—a deliberate pause in the questions. Ryker then asked the group how well they knew Erik Thompson. Looks were exchanged around the group, and then Nina spoke up. She told Ryker that Erik and Nadia had started dating in July that summer after meeting in one of their summer classes. Erik seemed like a great guy and appeared to really care for Nadia.

Erik and Nadia, as a couple, had gone camping and kayaking with the group along the Pictured Rocks in August. Erik and Nadia had also joined the group several times at the local pubs, once at a dance club, and at the annual UP beer festival in September held in Marquette. Nina told Ryker that Erik and Nadia, as a couple, were happy together and getting close. Erik had his own friends but was fitting in well with their oddball group. This caused chuckles around the table. Ryker smiled, nodded, and said, "Well, it takes all kinds."

Ryker was satisfied that the group wasn't hiding anything. These students were a close-knit group who had lost a good friend to suicide. Now a fellow student and friend of theirs was missing. As the detective finished talking to the group, he gave each of them one of his cards and told them to please call if they thought of something that might be helpful, no matter how trivial.

Caden and Nina watched as Ryker left the cafeteria. He was obviously known on campus and seemed to be well liked by students and staff. Ryker had approached a couple guys from the football team, slapped one of the jocks on the shoulder, and shook the hands of both. Smiles, comments, and a brief laugh were exchanged. Next, Ryker saw one of the college professors, said hello, and exchanged smiles and handshakes. The professor, whom Caden knew only by the university brochure, told Ryker to not be so scarce on campus and that he looked forward to seeing him at the next football game. With that, Detective Ryker was out the door, leaving the group exchanging questioning looks.

Troy started, "Do you guys think Nadia's suicide and Erik's disappearance have something in common?" Troy had just stated what they were all thinking. Obviously, the detective thought it possible. He hadn't come right out to say it, but his questions put all the connection lines out there. That wasn't hard to see.

Mingo spoke up. "Yep, Ryker was trying to connect the dots, all right, but Nadia's death was ruled a suicide by the coroner's office."

"Well, he obviously sees something that no one else is looking at," blurted Kat.

Troy spoke up now. "There it is again, that question why... Something is definitely not making sense here."

Caden scowled, slipping into his brooding "deep thinking" mode. Nina noticed and slipped her arm under his. Something about Nadia's suicide had just changed, but they couldn't tell exactly what it was.

Chapter 9

ADVENTURE-BOUND SCOUTS

Randy Adams and his wife, Amanda Adams, were group leaders for the local group Adventure Bound Scouts, an outdoor activity group for teens out of Crystal Falls. Both were teachers at the Crystal Falls High School and stayed involved with their son's activities. Reggie Townsend was a loan officer at the Crystal Falls Savings and Loan and had a son in the troop too. Reggie enjoyed working with the kids and was another troop leader for their group. Claire Peterson was a divorcee with a son in the troop and had been dating Reggie for three years. As of four months ago, Reggie and Claire were engaged and planned to be married the next summer.

The Adams couple, Reggie Townsend and Claire Peterson, all had a son in the Adventure Bound Scouts program. This group of scouts had been with the program for several years now and was working to become master scouts. All in all, there were the four adults and eight scouts in the group. One of the boys belonged to Randy and Amanda Adams, one boy to Reggie Townsend, one boy to Claire Peterson, and the other five from families around the western Upper Peninsula.

The two rental vans drove from the UP town of Crystal Falls, north on Highway 141, and then east on Highway 41/28 past Nestoria and to Craig Lake State Park in Ottawa National Forest. Craig Lake State Park would serve a base camp for the two weeks of this grand adventure to accomplish skills on the way to getting the coveted "master scout" title. From Craig Lake, the eight boys with two of their scout masters would drive to a trailhead to backpack on foot up into the McCormick Wilderness Area. Amanda Adams and Claire Townsend would remain at their base camp to track the group's progress and update local US Forest officials. The boys had outlined the scouting tasks and goals for their expedition. This would be an educational and survival trek into the Upper Peninsula's rugged wilderness area, a now protected area but an area filled with natural beauty and rich with a logging and mining heritage.

The goals of the scouts were ambitious. Not only would they be using their survival and woodcraft skills, but they would be documenting their trek for both task merits and publication. Their publications would vary but cover things such as assessing the state of conservation in the area and recommended future conservation efforts. Some of the backpacking route would be on an established trail system, and some would be cross-country doing map and compass orienteering. Their final leg would take them cross-country using map and compass to attempt to verify a purported abandoned mine shaft location.

With the guidance of Randy and Amanda Adams, the boys had coordinated with Michigan Technological University, the US Forest Service, the Michigan Department of Natural Resources, the Marquette sheriff's department, and the local Marquette emergency response teams. Preparation for the expedition even included contributions by Rosalie McCormick, present-day heir of Cyrus Hall McCormick, original owner of the original trek of land that would later be combined with another trek and be named the McCormick Wilderness Area.

Rosalie McCormick's great-grandfather was the first McCormick owner of the original 2,933 acres trek of land. Eventually, a McCormick heir (Gordon McCormick) willed the tract of land to the United States Department of Agriculture (USDA). The US Forest Service had management responsibility for the USDA and designated a tract of seventeen thousand acres, including the McCormick tract, as the McCormick Wilderness Area. This wilderness area would form the southwest boundary of the twenty-thousand-acre Huron Mountain Club. This expedition had to be carefully planned, coordinated, and executed with preplanned contingencies for emergencies. The survival and conservation tasks were normal fare for the Adventure Bound Scout merit task list. Locating the mine shaft, however, was a special request from Rosalie McCormick. In agreement to help document the long-lost and undocumented mine shaft site, Rosalie McCormick, now an elder woman in her mid-eighties, would make a donation to the Crystal Falls troop, thus providing funding for the venture and for similar activities for many years to come. The planning, preparation, and lead-up to the expedition were exciting for these young men and their mentors. Now, with the challenge to search for the mine shaft added, the expedition felt like a *real* adventure. Maybe they would even end up on National Geographic. Rosalie McCormick, however, saw her investment as a subtle way to find something long lost to the pages of time and her family history—the Astor side of her family history.

Randy Adams and Reggie Townsend were friends and had been since their high school days at Crystal Falls. Both were athletic outdoorsmen and survival experts in their own right. Randy had attended Michigan Tech in Houghton to get his degree in the mineral and mining sciences, while Reggie had gone to NMU in Marquette to get his degree in finance and banking. After college, Randy and Reggie, along with Randy's fiancée at the time, Amanda, would spend a year in Colorado going through the Outward Bound program, first as students and then as instructors. Those were good times, but they didn't pay the bills. So after a year of running around in the mountains of Colorado, they returned home to Crystal Falls and worked.

The experience at Outward Bound for Randy and Amanda was life-changing and led them in the direction of a career change, that of teaching. Randy had planned on working in the UP mining industry, but jobs were tough with a downturn in the UP's mining economy. Amanda's degree was in mineral sciences, too, but the job market had changed. Teaching jobs always seemed to be in demand somewhere, and the experience with Outward Bound made them realize that they both loved teaching. It was pretty much a no-brainer after that, and it was simply a matter of taking a little more schooling to get a teaching certificate and a job. Life was good for Randy and Amanda, and they were both excited to watch their boy Rob as he became a fine young man and soon a master scout with the ABS program.

It didn't take long to get base camp set up at the Craig Lake State Park campground. Already one of the US Forest rangers had stopped by to check things out and get briefed up on the troop's plan. Tony Lindeman was the US Forest Service ranger assigned to monitor the troop. Tony had been an Eagle Scout with the Boy Scouts and had volunteered when the district supervisor talked about the Adventure Bound scout project in one of their weekly meetings back in early August.

The monitoring job really didn't entail much effort on the part of forest ranger Tony Lindeman—check in with Amanda and Claire by phone once daily to get an update of the progress of the troop, maybe give some advice, and, if needed, assist with any emergency. Tony Lindeman had backpacked into the McCormick Wilderness Area two or three times a year, so he was familiar with a lot of the area, especially the trails. Once a year, usually late springtime after the snow melted, he and a few other forest rangers would backpack in to clear and clean up trails. Other times he would pack in to check on overdue backpacker or, as in one case, recover the body of a lost hunter whom they had discovered had fallen off a cliff and died.

After verifying routes, time lines, and telephone numbers and wishing the scout troop good luck, forest ranger Tony Lindeman drove away from the base camp. It was reassuring to the adults that they had a good plan and solid contingencies for any emergencies. Claire had heated up a supper of canned beef stew in a large kettle on the Coleman gas stove. The boys were all hungry and anxious to get on with the expedition. Tonight, though, they enjoyed the comforts of not having to boil their water and having a two-seater outhouse with soft toilet paper. In the morning, they would eat breakfast, finish packing their gear into fifty pounds of *essentials*, and get hauled up to the trailhead in the vans before beginning the hike into the bush. The boys were upbeat and excited. This would be an adventure to remember…in more ways than one.

Chapter 10

PHILANTHROPIST

Four hundred miles away, in Wheaton, Illinois, Rosalie McCormick was gazing out her upstairs window of the McCormick cottage. The English-style cottage was actually a mansion, meticulously nestled in the five-hundred-acre Cantigny Estate. The view made Rosalie smile as she scanned the gardens and grounds, which were beautiful as always.

Rosalie McCormick had just returned from the military museum, named after her grandfather, Colonel Robert R. McCormick. At a spry age of only eighty-five, Rosalie McCormick was mentally as sharp as ever, physically active, and still spearheading the McCormick philanthropy projects. From her commanding view of the grounds in her second-story window, the rose gardens made a stark contrast to the WWI tanks and artillery pieces lined up outside the Colonel Robert R. McCormick First Division Museum. Nonetheless, the family estate grounds were as magnificent as always. The colonel would be proud of her for keeping his legacy so immaculate.

The McCormicks' Cantigny Estate was a popular site for thousands of visitors each year and also served as a secluded off-site meeting place for the "old money" Chicago financial elites.

Rosalie turned her gaze to the large wall in her upstairs office. The room was ornate, rich with stained, carved oak, valuable paintings, marble statues and with a large antique oak desk positioned as if to say "in charge" of everything in the room. This was her thinking room, or war room as her grandfather, Colonel McCormick, liked to refer to it as when he was still alive. Behind the ancient oak desk was her working wall. She would post, tape, draw, write, or pin the thoughts and ideas racing through her gray-hair-covered head. She would capture, organize, and prioritize her thoughts like her father and grandfather had taught her.

Rosalie had four different "project spaces" set up on her white board. Admittedly, she thought the board looked strangely out of place compared to the rest of the ornate room decor. For the moment, however, she was focused on the project space labeled "Mine—UP." Various printouts of old articles, old surveys, old documents—faded and ancient—littered the part of the board she scrutinized with care. Her brow furrowed with thought as her eyes danced from one paper to another. They were pieces to a puzzle to her. Rosalie loved solving puzzles.

In the morning, Rosalie McCormick would make phone calls from her to-do list. She would call Tony Lindeman in Marquette for an update on the Adventure Bound scout troop heading into the McCormick wilderness area. Then she would call Professor Scott Brunberry at Michigan Tech in Houghton and get an update on the papers he had discovered, which hinted at a long forgotten or lost gold mine. While she was at it, she would ask how her grandson, Dirk Astor was doing. She was hoping that the rape charges, which got him kicked out of Yale, were still *lost* from any student records making it to Michigan Tech in Houghton. God knows enough money was paid to make the charges go away. Michigan Tech was just the kind of out-of-the-way school needed to let the news cycle die out and protect the family name. She would have to figure out a subtle way to quiz Professor Brunberry without drawing any unwanted attention to her grandson's *extracurricular* activities.

After the brief *side thought* of her grandson Dirk, Rosalie's thoughts went back to the original reason to talk with Brunberry—the possible mine location. The exact location of the mine shaft was sketchy from the records Professor Brunberry discovered. As best as he could figure, the mine could be located very near the border of the original McCormick UP property, the Huron Mountain Club, and a tract that had belonged to the US government. Last week, she was able to verify that the McCormick estate has retained mineral rights to property of the original McCormick 2,933 acres when it was deeded to the US Department of Agriculture. The question she had now was, is the mine—if there is a mine—on the original McCormick tract, the Huron Mountain Tact, or the old US Government tact? She needed to know in case survey documents needed to be corrected.

More payoffs, but what a grand puzzle! she thought to herself.

Chapter 11

CLUELESS IN MARQUETTE

Detective Stannis Ryker sat at his deck in the Marquette police department, staring blankly at his office phone. Mrs. Thompson had just called, crying and pleading with him. He felt completely useless and was unable to give Erik Thompson's mother any good news. Erik had been missing for over a week now. No tips, no anonymous calls, no activity on credit cards…nothing. It was as if Erik Thompson just dropped off the face of the earth. What few clues he had gathered from interviews of Erik's friends and other students all turned out to be dead ends. The only possible person whom he thought would know where he was, well, she was dead, and that would be Nadia Red Horse. Ryker set the phone down.

Ryker didn't like getting his ass chewed out by the chief of police. Ryker was a competent cop, and he understood the chief was just letting him know that pressure was coming from all directions—the press, the parents, and the administration at NMU. A missing student didn't fare well for the confidence of a community like Marquette, with a population of almost 22,000. The city has a low crime rate, so it didn't take much to shake up community confidence. News outlets were starting to pick up the story of missing Erik Thompson, downstate, into Wisconsin, and into Minnesota. In one respect, that was good; they were getting the word out. On the other hand, it also meant that the clock was ticking and the situation was getting dire.

Detective Pete Shelby approached Ryker's desk and sat down in an empty metal chair. Shelby had been assigned to team up with

Ryker now that things were getting sensitive with the community and parents.

Shelby was new to the department, having moved there from New York, and was still getting settled in to life in the Upper Peninsula. Shelby had a big city air about him that Ryker didn't care for. It was kind of a "better than thou" attitude, but he kept it in check. Ryker could work with just about anyone; the military and team sports taught him that. There was just something about Shelby that Ryker couldn't quite put his finger on. *Something just under the big city facade...probably nothing. I would just have to live with it,* Ryker thought to himself.

"Anything?" Shelby asked Ryker.

Ryker shook his head no. "Nope, nothing but more questions... oh, and ass-chewing from the chief."

Shelby laughed. "Ya, he took a couple pounds off mine too." They both laughed.

Ryker and Shelby went down their list of latest interviews and findings, comparing notes and trying to find something, anything, to give them a clue as to what might have happened to Erik Thompson. Between the two of them, all they had was a big fat nothing sandwich. Yep, they were clueless and they needed a break in the case... anything to get them on a scent.

The two detectives were now working with the sheriff's department, the Michigan State Police, and the tribal police. The tribal police had been Ryker's idea because Erik Thompson's girlfriend had been tribal. "No rock unturned, as they say," Ryker said out loud to no one in particular. Their web was expanding as they started to bring more resources to the hunt for Eric Thompson. "Something had to break loose soon, I can feel it," Ryker finally said.

The two detectives agreed to circle back on the some of the interviews to see if any stories changed or maybe someone remembered something. Ryker would drive down to L'Anse, link up the tribal cops, and talk to Mr. and Mrs. Red Horse again. Then he would head back to the neighborhood where Nadia Red Horse had lived and knock on a few more doors. Shelby would contact the campus police and would go onto NMU grounds to talk to all of

Erik Thompson's professors. He would then head up to the Huron Mountain Club and talk to some of the resident workers. He was told that occasionally, some of the "ritzys" from Huron Mountain Club would come into town, meet up with locals, and party. Shelby said he had a few contacts at the Huron Mountain Club, so Ryker thought it was a good idea to have Detective Shelby do the club. Ryker didn't know any of the members of the Huron Mountain Club, but several he had met seemed to be real jerks.

Chapter 12

WEEKEND PLAN

Caden and Mingo were having lunch together at the main campus cafeteria; it was Wednesday. They had just finished a run together. They had managed to squeeze in a run and a short weightlifting workout after their morning classes.

Caden was hungry and was scarfing down his food hardly taking a breath. Mingo laughed at him. "You aren't in Ranger School, man. You can chew your food before you swallow it!"

Caden about choked mid-bite as he looked at the expression on Mingo's face. "What, like you've never inhaled a meal before?" They both laughed. They had both gone through Ranger School together while assigned to the Second Ranger Battalion in the state of Washington at Joint Base Lewis-McChord. Ranger School taught you how to eat fast—that was their joke. Both coming from Michigan had been their first connection. Attending the same Ranger class and surviving multiple combat tours in the same squad had made them close, "blood brother" close.

"You know we still haven't gone hunting yet this fall?" Caden said. Mingo nodded his head in acknowledgment. It was now Mingo inhaling his food—old habits. "Uncle Jake invited us down to his place to hunt, you know?" Caden continued as he wiped his mouth with the paper napkin and finished the last of his Gatorade drink.

"We should go," Mingo responded.

"Let's make a long weekend of it. Kat and Nina will want to go, but Troy and Syd...probably not," Caden answered back.

"Yep, they would rather study or go hiking than hunt." Mingo smirked. Hunting was in Mingo's blood, and it was tradition. For Caden, hunting was in his blood, too, and a family tradition. Fall and the changing season always brought out the irresistible urge to be in the woods and get back to the natural order of things.

Referring to Troy and Syd's preference not to hunt, Caden retorted with a smirk, "We are not all stone-cold killers like you, Mingo." They both laughed. Afghanistan and Iraq had seen plenty of killing by both of them. It wasn't something they were particularly proud of, but it is what it is. They had killed the enemy during combat operations. Sometimes with a rifle or sidearm. Sometimes with a sniper rifle. Sometimes calling in artillery or an air strike. Sometimes with a knife or their bare hands in hand-to-hand combat. It was kill or be killed, that's just the way it was, the nature of things during war.

Campus life often gave Caden a chance to "ponder life," as he liked to call of it. War gives a person a lot to ponder. He thought that maybe man's connection with nature was being bred out or brainwashed out with modern society, as it seemed like it was in America these days. The attitude of people, especially universities, with their safe spaces, identity politics, gender dictionary, politically correct bullshit, and intolerance of conservative views was something he just couldn't relate to. Mingo saw it, too, and they had long philosophical talks about it on occasion, usually after they had a couple beers. Mingo was tied to his native people's traditions, though, so he liked to remind Caden it was a "White guy" thing. Caden would always laugh and ask when he could become the token White guy in the tribe. "Anytime you want brother" was Mingo's normal response. Insulting each other, for military guys, was more of an expression of close friendship rather than a demeaning slur. That was something "snowflake liberals" would never understand about the military guys.

Their conversation went from talking about hunting to making plans for the weekend to the recent interview with Detective Pete Shelby. Shelby was the new guy assigned to the missing person case of Erik Thompson. Apparently, Shelby was partnering up with Detective Ryker. It seemed that Shelby was circling back on Ryker's interviews to see if there had been any new revelations or "jogged memories." This time, however, Shelby was interviewing the students one-on-one, probably verifying stories from the first interview with Ryker—at least that's what Caden guessed. Erik Thompson's disappearance was still a big empty goose egg to the detectives. Now, it appeared, they were changing up their strategy and leaning on a hunch that maybe the Nadia Red Horse suicide and Erik Thompson's disappearance were somehow connected. The two incidents, being somehow connected, had been something in the back of Caden's mind, and he had mentioned it to their group a couple times during supper. It didn't make sense, and there was nothing to connect the two—that is, except for the fact that Nadia's suicide or Erik's disappearance made no sense.

At supper that evening, hunting plans were made to head down to Jake and Susan Catrin's place for a weekend of hunting. Caden, Mingo, Kat, and Nina would go. Troy and Sydney, as predicted, would remain in Marquette to catch up on studying and do some more research on a project the two of them were working on.

"Does the project involve a wrestling match between the sheets?" Kat laughed. The red expressions and guilty looks on Troy and Sydney's faces told it all.

Caden came to their rescue. "It's cool…not like we didn't know already, anyway, especially the way you two have been acting lately. And you don't need our permission, you know."

Syd seemed to make an outward sigh of relief. She was always the shy one. Troy, on the other hand, burst out laughing. "Way to go, Kat. You officially let the *cat* out of the bag." Kat had already known because Sydney had already confided in her. Even in the small tight group, there were secrets. Kat didn't see the point in trying to hide this one; after all, Syd and Troy were great together and made a *cute* couple.

The rest of the week passed quickly. Friday, by noon, Caden, Mingo, Nina, and Kat were packed, loaded, and pulling out of the parking lot of their apartment complex heading south toward Jake and Susan Catrin's five-hundred-acre property. Caden's black Toyota Tacoma was packed and ready to go. The double cab pickup truck was loaded with four people and a duffel bag in the passenger compartments. The back pickup bed, covered with a locking Leer topper, had suitcases and gear stuffed to the brim. It was only a weekend, but hunting gear took up the most space.

The ride from Marquette to Schoolcraft County was enjoyable with the sunny sky and rich fall colors. Callie Catrin... Kat...was looking forward to seeing her mom and dad and also hunting. Caden and Mingo were looking forward to hunting. Nina was looking forward to the hunting, but moreover, she was looking forward to a weekend of quality time with Caden and away from their hectic student schedule.

The Catrin property was Jake and Susan's dream property. After thirty-four years of bouncing around the globe, extended periods of deployment separation, they both wanted a place to set roots and call home. This was it, their dream property. Five hundred acres surrounded by thousands of acres of Hiawatha National Forest. It was just the kind of "elbow room" Jake Catrin needed. The property had a small wildlife lake, a stream with brook trout, rolling high ground with hardwoods, some cedar swamp, and a few agriculture fields. The main lodge was meticulously constructed with whole logs and panned out 3,200 square feet plus two massive decks. The lodge sat upon a high point of the property with a fifteen-acre opening. The open space had a small garden and two small apple orchards.

Back inside the lodge, the great room had a cathedral ceiling with a magnificent stone fireplace with an ornate carved half log mantle. The stone of the fireplace was glacier rolled granite and rose an impressive two stories from floor to roof.

Out on the property grounds, the small lake was accessible by a dirt two track, which led up to a small two-bedroom log cabin nestled neatly with a view of the shoreline. The cabin was small, but it was built with the same care and craftsmanship as the main lodge. Jake Catrin made sure of that.

After warm welcomes and hugs, the *kids* started to unload the Tacoma and get settled in for a weekend of relaxation. Kate, of course, had her bedroom upstairs. Nina was assigned Caden's old bedroom at the opposite end of the upstairs hallway. The two *boys* had a choice of staying in the other two spare bedrooms upstairs, opposite each other, or staying out at the lake cabin. At least those were Susan Catrin's room assignment. Whether the *kids* decided to abide by her plan remained to be seen. The cabin was always a favorite spot when either Kat or Caden had friends over for company.

Chapter 13

ISLAND LAKE

Adventure Bound group leaders Randy Adams and Reggie Townsend were proud of how well the boys in the troop were holding up and pleased with their progress. After being dropped off at the west gate entrance to the McCormick Wilderness Area, they began the trek on foot. The west gate entrance was located about ten miles past the Peshekee River, after the town of Champion. It was day four into the expedition, and they had already made their way north up the McCormick main trail to White Deer Lake and were now heading cross-country through rugged terrain, crossing from Marquette County into Baraga County. The goal for that night was to make it to the old camp 36, which was somewhere between Clear Lake and Island Lake, and set up camp. So far, the weather had been good to them, and everyone was in excellent condition, with no injuries or sickness.

Their visit to White Deer Lake had been amazing. With a little imagination, it was like stepping back in time. As they were coming up to the lake, there were still traces of the old boathouse. Out on the island, there were still traces of Chimney Cabin, Beaver Cabin, Birch Cabin, Library Cabin, and Living Room Cabin. The troop had the old maps, pictures, and drawing to compare. They took digital photographs of building foundations, scrap metal left from old vehicles, anything that could document what was once there, and now the recovery of the land by Mother Nature.

Thinking back to the times when Cyrus McCormick built the roads, trails, cabins, and facilities for White Deer Lake, one could gain a true appreciation of how rugged our forefathers were to purge into this wilderness area. Of course, before McCormick, there were the lumber barons and mining moguls who would strip this land of all its timber. Back in the nineteenth and early twentieth centuries, a time when the land was raped and pillaged with no disregard for the aftermath, the "captains of industry" would fill their ledgers with profits and wealth while the men and women at the bottom of the food chain would sweat, bleed, toil, and, in some cases, die for meager wages.

The fact that the rich and powerful hadn't actually done the backbreaking labor in this rugged wilderness area wasn't lost on the boys. Even now as they enjoyed this adventure and toiled under their backpacks, they realized that it was a McCormick who was providing the funding for this scouting enterprise and them doing all the work. Not that they were complaining, but it did seem ironic in a historic and cruel sort of way.

It was slow going now. The group was working their way through rugged steep rocks for a while and then around wet bogs for the next piece of the trek. This was true rugged wilderness in all its grueling glory. The boys were tracking their route and progress with their maps and compasses. Group leader Randy Adams had a GPS, but it was turned off and stuffed in his backpack. He liked working with his map and compass. "On track," he said to himself as he looked at his topo map and scanned the terrain features. Randy's fellow scout leader, Reggie Townsend, carried his GPS and watched their progress on the topo screen of the handheld device. "On track." He nodded to Randy, who was near the front of the single-file caravan of human pack mules.

About once every one or two hours, the group would stop. The scout leaders would go to each scout and have them point out where they were on the topo map each one carried. Each boy was proving to be exceptional at orienteering. They would point out terrain features they had passed and point out terrain features in view of their current location. Using intersections and resections with their map, compass, and protractor, they would plot azimuths on their maps and determine exactly their location on the map. Randy and

Reggie were pleased with each scout. Their classroom instruction and backwoods orienteering course lessons were absorbed by these young minds. They could see the confidence growing in each of the boys with every stop and map check.

Toiling with their backpacks had its rewards. The group came across deer tracks, bear tracks, wolf tracks, and even a set of moose tracks. It was exciting reading the tracks, and land was bringing a whole new dimension to *sight* for the scouts. This new sight was a closer understanding of the natural world that most kids won't get from reading a book, playing a video game, or even playing sports. These young scouts were learning to decode the secrets of this sheet of paper with all its squiggly lines and colors. With a good topographic map, the mind could walk the terrain, anticipate obstacles, and find points of interest—all without even having set foot on the ground.

The group was moving along quietly now. They had seen the rewards and thrills of moving like ghosts through the bush. At one point, just northwest of White Deer Lake and after Castle Rock lookout, the group peeked over a ridge and came upon an albino buck browsing on acorns in the valley below. Obviously, some of the gene pool of the albino deer, who was the namesake for White Deer Lake, had survived and been passed on. The boys had managed to get some pictures of the deer; they knew it would be important and something that Rosalie McCormick would enjoy seeing. The experience of seeing the white deer had been a mystic, almost religious, experience for the group of scouts. They knew, of course, the white buffalo had significance in Native American culture, and they were sure a white buck did too. That was something they would do more research on when writing their memoirs of the expedition. In European hunting culture, they knew the white stag of Saint Hubertus, the patron saint of hunters, was a defining moment in the sainthood of the bishop. The experience of seeing the white buck was a good omen for them.

Finding the remnants to old camp 36 was easy, though there wasn't really anything remaining except a few rotted boards with rusty nails and pieces of an old-time camp stove, once used to heat an outfitter-style tent. There was a small clearing with a good view of the island on Island Lake. This would be the perfect spot to pitch camp. For the past couple days, one military-style, freeze-dried meal per day was the meal schedule. This was the lead-in to the survival tasks. This camp would provide an opportunity to wash and dry out socks, catch some fish, and do a little small game hunting. All fires would be made without matches. This was the spot for a couple days of rest, and it was also the place for working on the survival skills merit tasks. The boys energetically set into action, building their individual survival shelters, prioritizing tasks, and enjoying the relief of not having the backpacks pulling on their shoulders.

Chapter 14

FALL HARVEST

Fall harvest
Catrin property, Schoolcraft County

Callie Catrin—Kat—was perched up almost twenty feet up in an ancient oak tree. Kat was dressed in camouflage and she had green and brown face paint covering the highlights on her face. The small platform with seat, which she was using as her perch, was solid and quiet. It was a Lone Wolf tree stand with a metal ladder secured to the tree for the climb up. *This was much better than a seat in a college classroom*, Kat thought to herself.

Kat began moving to stand up now very slowly and very quietly. She held the bow in her left hand and with her right hand held the release. The mechanical release was anchored taunt to the nocking point on bow drawstring. Her eyes were following the buck, which seemed to magically appear in the thick timber. The deer, she could see, was now working its way toward the forest edge and the small apple orchard. Her dad had strategically planted that orchard years ago, exactly for moments like this. The small orchard of twelve trees stood in ranks about forty yards out into the open field.

Kat could feel her heart pumping hard with adrenaline now. The buck was just inside the tree line, standing there, looking, smelling, checking for any danger. A few steps more by the buck, which Kat could now see was a nice eight point, and he would be in the open field. From her position, Kat would have a broadside seventeen-yard shot. She took a slow deep breath in to calm herself. The buck flagged its tail side to side. She knew the buck was going to move now. As it passed behind a small spruce tree, she drew her bow. Four steps out into the open and Kat whispered out a subtle faun bleat. The buck froze, unsure where the noise came from. Kat focused her twenty-yard pin just below mid-body on the deer and slightly behind the shoulder. A double-lung shot was what she wanted. She squeezed the trigger on the mechanical release, and the arrow flew true.

The buck jumped and sprinted thirty yards before slowing to a walk. He didn't even know what just happened. The buck weakly walked another ten yards, began to stagger, and then fell and expired. Kat could just barely make out the buck through the trees as it went down. This was Kat's third buck and her biggest so far. She let out a long sigh of relief and let her heart race as she sat down in her perch to enjoy the view. She wanted to savor the moment and sit for a while to let the animal expire before she worked her way down the tree to the ground.

Thirty minutes later, on another corner of the Catlin property, Nina would arrow a nice seven-point buck. Nina had already harvested her share of deer by the age of twenty-one—many with a rifle and many with bow and arrow. Nina loved hunting, and archery hunting was her favorite. That was another thing she and Caden had in common—the love of archery hunting and hunting in general. Nina was pleased with herself. She had made a good shot and she was excited to tell Caden and the rest of the group.

Jake Catlin used the side-by-side four-wheeler to help the girls recover their bucks and haul them to the shed where the deer would be hung up and cooled before being processed for the freezer. Nina and Kat had already finished gutting their bucks and had them hanging by the time Caden and Mingo made it back from their evening tree stand vigil. It was dark now, and the light to the hanging shed was on. Kat, Nina, Jake, and Susan were standing there admiring the deer and talking about the hunt.

Jake saw them first as Caden and Mingo approached the light. "No blood on the hands, no missing or bloody arrows in the quiver… let me guess, you guys had a good nap in your stands." Uncle Jake was going to have fun with this. Both of the girls got bucks on the first evening hunt, and the boys got "skunked." Caden and Mingo both smiled; they knew Jake was going to work this one for all it was worth. The boys stepped into the shed where both Kat and Nina were beaming from ear to ear. "Nice job!" Caden said as he looked at the unquestionable smiles of success on Kat and Nina. Mingo was going to go on offense, though, as he looked at the bucks.

"Jake, I didn't know you wanted us to shoot small bucks here."

Kat punched Mingo in shoulder. "Ya right, mister." They all laughed and then exchanged brief reports of deer seen and shots passed up. After a few minutes of lively talk, they headed up to the main lodge to get some of Susan's home cooking—a nice change from cafeteria food. Nina hung playfully on Caden's shoulder as they walked. Caden held her around the waist and kept giving her kisses of congratulations. Kat pushed Mingo in the shoulder and raced him up to the porch leading to the front door. Life was good at the Catlin lodge.

Fall harvest
Island Lake, McCormick Wilderness Area

At the camp on Island Lake in the McCormick Wilderness Area, the group of Adventure Bound Scouts relished the smell of fresh-caught pike sizzling in a frying pan over a bed of hot coals. The squirrel stew with an assortment of wild mushrooms, wild chives, and cattail roots was simmering in the tin pot hanging over the fire. The once-a-day freeze-dried meals were good but left a big void in the stomachs of active young men who were used to three meals a day. The self-imposed hunger diet was part of the survival exercise. The scouts needed to feel the hunger to get the true sense of survival. This wild game meal was going to be a special treat.

They had all eaten wild game before—venison, small game like rabbits, squirrel, and grouse. As for fish, they had eaten just about every game fish known to Michigan lakes and streams. This meal of wild game, however, was special. The meal was fresh from nature's shopping cart, and a little dirt or ashes wouldn't matter or deter them from eating all of it, especially with the ravaging appetites boiling in the stomachs of the scouts.

As the group enjoyed the warmth of the fire and full bellies, a quiet contentment came over their faces as dancing flames highlighted facial features and confident smiles. These boys were becoming men. The hard-fought lessons of trekking into this wilderness area were revealing and enlightening. The experience was doing exactly what was intended. It was a transformational experience. Self-sacrifice, self-discipline, hard work, and nature's lessons were all bringing forth the man in each boy.

In the distance, a lone wolf began to howl. Soon it was joined by several other wolves. The distant howling continued and seemed to converge to one wolf. Then silence. No words were spoken around the campfire as the young men listened intently to the choir of wolves. It was amazing, almost magical, to be part of this wonderful thing called nature. The troop wasn't just reading about nature or hearing about it from some talking head narrating on a TV screen. These young men were living it. The manifestation and man's place in nature, his responsibility to it, was taking form in the minds of each young lad. This wilderness experience would serve as a building block to the character of each boy in becoming a man. Each scout seemed to be occupied with inner reflection as the campfire flames danced and cast their symphony of shadows, crackling, and warmth. Randy Adams and Reggie Townsend scanned through the deep thought expressions on each of the scouts around the fire. They felt good and they were proud of these young men. Life was good for the Adventure Bound Scout troop from Crystal Falls.

Fall harvest
White Deer Lake, McCormick Wilderness Area

The wolf pack had picked up the scent of the young deer a while back. It was dark now, and the wolves were closing in on the scent. The albino yearling and its mother had managed to outpace the pack, but the wolves were relentless in the pursuit; hunger had a way of doing that. The pack had finally managed to separate the younger deer from its mother; it was just a matter of time and persistence now.

Members of the pack were flanking the deer on each side, while others stayed on the track scent. Finally, the pack had trapped the hapless deer in a small canyon with no way out. In the darkness of the forest, the white deer almost glowed, and the predators could pick it out easily as it tried to hide among the trees and brush. That was one reason why albinos didn't tend to survive long in the wild. They did not possess the natural camouflage developed over the millennium through natural selection and survival of the fittest.

The pack moved in for the kill. The deer hadn't broken cover yet. Suddenly, in a white flash, the deer leapt and dodged desperately to outmaneuver the attacking wolves. It was useless. Each wolf was larger than the deer and had experience taking down many prey animals, including deer.

As quickly as the deer broke cover, one wolf latched onto a hind leg. The second wolf would grasp the deer by the throat. The rest of the pack moved in, tearing the still live deer apart while it bleated in terror. Within a few brief minutes, the bleating had stopped. All that was left now was the snarling of the wolves as they fought, tugged, and tore into this once beautiful creature.

Life was good for the wolves…not so good for the albino deer.

Fall harvest
Boarder of Huron Mountain Club and McCormick Wilderness Area

On the border of the Huron Mountain Club property and the McCormick Wilderness Area, a large antlered beast stood atop a high rocky cliff. The beast was massive as the moonlight reflected on its terrifying horror. The head was that of a great antlered wolf beast. It stood upright with long edgy claws attached to fingers and strong muscled arms. Those, in turn, were attached to a muscled body covered in raggedy, mangy hair. The beast's eyes glowed of pure evil, peering down to the bottom of the cliff. There lay the lifeless, half-eaten body of Erick Thompson. The body was crumpled in the rocks and still had remnants of shredded clothing on it. The clothing, what was left of it, appeared to be hunting attire—brown canvas pants, hiking boots, a red flannel shirt, and an orange hunting vest…at least what was left.

Erik's lifeless body lay mangled from the impact of being tossed off the cliff onto the boulders. His skull was crushed, and his body and limbs were bent in unnatural positions from the headlong toss by the beast. The rest of Erik's shredded flesh and clothing were the result of slashing claws and gnashing teeth. Standing at the top of the cliff, the great beast's popping jaws of death were still dripping with blood and pieces of shredded flesh. The monster tilted its head back, letting out an unearthly screaming howl followed by a loud guttural roar in the direction of the moon. The great beast, or Wendigo as it was known in Indian tribal legend, then disappeared into the shadowy darkness of one of Michigan's last wilderness areas. In a short time, a few days perhaps, Erik's mangled body would become carrion for turkey vultures, ravens, crows, and insects. Now both Erik Thompson and Nadia Red Horse would join the ranks of the dead victims and the Huron Mountain's ghosts of the past.

Evil had taken both Erik and Nadia. Nadia's death had been less gruesome but nonetheless gruesome and just as dead. A couple weeks before, Erik had been beaten up and chased off into the darkness of the Huron Mountains. Nadia, who had been drugged senseless, was brutally raped and strangled. Under the cover of darkness, her lifeless body was cleaned up and taken back to her little white house with black trim and staged to make it look like a suicide. Dirk Astor's henchmen were good at cleaning up after him because they had lots of practice. After all, they were experts at this sort of thing, and that's why they were on the payroll.

Chapter 15

CAMPFIRES STORIES

Stars twinkled and ebbed in the clear black October night sky. Even the crackling campfire and crescent moon couldn't steal the wonder from those countless stars.

The cabin looked like a painted picture with the calm lake and reflections of the moon and stars set as a backdrop. This was why the lake cabin on the Catrin property was such a favorite place to stay. It was breathtaking in its picturesque beauty, especially around a nighttime campfire.

Caden and Nina sat on a blanket, folded as a cushion on the ground. Caden was leaning back against a huge log that served as both backrest and campfire seat. Nina sat between Caden's legs, using him as her backrest and holding his arms that were wrapped comfortably around her torso. Nina's face shined a content smile as she gazed into the dancing flames of the fire. Caden's expression was calm and content, too, and he nuzzled Nina's neck and breathed in her scent. He could feel his loins begin to stir, so he took another sip of beer and turned his attention back to Mingo, who was talking about Native American legends of the Upper Peninsula.

Kat's expression was priceless as she sat tensely on the log that Caden was leaning back against. She wasn't sure if Mingo was bull-shitting the group or talking about real Native American legends and stories. Uncle Jake and Aunt Susan had joined the *kids* at the lake cabin and were watching Kat's expressions with some amusement.

Supper had been wonderful…again. This Saturday evening, it was roast beef, mashed potatoes, corn on the cob, and freshly made apple pie. The pie was made from apples collected off the trees of the small apple orchard near where Nina had arrowed her buck Friday evening.

Both Nina and Kat had declined to hunt the morning and evening today, Saturday. Instead, they chose to sleep in and then take Jake and Susan into Manistique to get a late breakfast at the Cedar Street Café, opting for one of their famous "garbage omelets."

After the late breakfast, the four decided to walk it off by doing a little moseying around at a couple of the local shops. The Mustard Seed and Top O' Lake Sport Shop store always had something of interest. Manistique was one of those quaint, picturesque, Victorian-era, historical harbor towns on Lake Michigan. The Victorian-style town was reminiscent of the booming lumber and mining times of the late 1800s in Michigan. Manistique had a friendly, traditional, laid-back feel to it, typical of most small towns in the Upper Peninsula. After the trip to town, they all went back to the Catlin lodge to hang out, relax, and wait for Caden and Mingo to finish their evening hunt.

*****

Mingo had just finished telling the story of how French trappers had first come into the area of Manistique and established a small trading post in the place where the Seul Choix Pointe Lighthouse (pronounced "sish wa") was now located. Jake and Susan Catrin watched Mingo with fascination and interest, amazed once again that Mingo, who very rarely said a lot, seemed to be a walking encyclopedia of local Native American history.

Kat's expression was less skeptical now. "Okay, I can see that, but is it true that if you drink porcupine piss, it will help you get a buck, like in the movie *Escanaba in Da Moonlight* with Jeff Daniels? You know, so Nina and I don't have to start calling you and Caden the buckless Yoopers!" There was another jab at Caden and Mingo, who once again opted to pass on a couple smaller bucks, thus getting "skunked" again.

Caden was in mid-sip of his freshly opened beer and almost spit it all over the back of Nina's head. Kat's little outburst was completely unexpected. Luckily, he turned his head just in time to save Nina from the beer-filled explosion of a choking laugh. Jake and Susan burst out in a feverish laugh. Nina would have laughed, except for the near miss from Caden. Mingo, on the other hand, sat on his log stump seat, completely expressionless. He had never seen the movie *Escanaba in Da Moonlight*, so he sat somewhat dumbfounded and clueless. Kat was in charge of Indian legends now—of her own Indian legends—and she loved seeing the expression on Mingo's face.

Mingo, looking for some help, glanced at Caden, who was now in control of his laugh. Caden smiled a pitiful smile back at poor clueless Mingo, who seemed to be taking the blunt of Kat's little prank. Callie, Kat, explained the highlights of the movie and how one of the main characters, Reuben Soady, played by Jeff Daniels, was married to the character Wolf Moon Dance Soady, played by Kimberly Norris-Guerrero. Kat went on to talk about Reuben, "Despite being married to Wolf Moon, his Native American wife, he was the buckless Yooper—the nickname given to him for never having shot a buck and because it looked like he was cursed. Mingo held a straight face even after Caden's honest smile, not knowing whether Kat was joking or not.

Kat went on explaining that the movie was a comedy, which exaggerated some common "Yooperisms" and took a lot of liberal comic freedoms with Native American culture and traditions. Kat continued explaining, getting to her porcupine piss comment, that Wolf Moon gave Reuben a traditional tribal recipe and ritual that would end his "buckless" curse. That recipe and ritual involved drinking a concoction with porcupine urine as a key ingredient. It also involved sprinkling the solution all over the person with the bad luck.

Mingo looked around the circle of friends at the campfire, waiting for another round of laughs, but saw that Caden nodded. Apparently, Kat was on the level, and there was such a movie as *Escanaba in Da Moonlight*. Finally, Mingo asked, "Did it work?" Another round of laughs started, and this time, Mingo was laughing with the group.

"Yes," Kat replied. "And we brought you some of that special juice so we don't have to start calling you a buckless Yooper. Kat popped a beer can top and handed it to Mingo. Again, another round of chuckles.

Mingo looked into the fire again and said, “You know, as I think about it, there may be some truth to that. A toast to Kat and Nina’s bucks!”

With that, Jake and Susan finished off their beers and took a leave from their group of *kids* around the campfire. “Well, time for the older folks to call it a night,” Jake proclaimed as they hugged each of them—Kat, Caden, Nina, and Mingo—in turn. Jake gave Mingo a reassuring wink and left the group to the warmth of the fire. Jake and Susan then climbed into the side-by-side and drove the trail back to the main lodge, the headlights forming a light tunnel through the dark void in the trees, finally disappearing and leaving only darkness.

For a while, the group just enjoyed the campfire and solitude of the lake cabin. Nina got up and stretched, and Kat poked a stick in the fire, moving a couple half-burned logs into a better position. Mingo set a couple newly split pieces of wood in the fire, and Caden stepped into the shadows to take a leak.

When the group reassembled at positions by the fire, Nina and Caden were sitting on the log bench while Kat and Mingo took up positions on upright log seats. It seemed like the night was winding down as everyone sat in silence. For the moment, everyone was back to their individual thoughts, simply enjoying the quiet and presence of one another’s company.

Nina was the one who finally broke the silence. “Syd and Troy would have really enjoyed this,” she said, but her face was expressing something deeper. Slow nods of agreement passed around the group.

“I really miss Nadia,” Nina whispered, a single tear forming in the corner of her eye and finally trailing over her high cheekbone and down her face. Caden put his hand on Nina’s leg, and she held his arm with both of hers, wrapping under his arm and pulling close.

Caden and Mingo continued staring into the fire as if there was something about to appear from the yellow, red, and white flames. “I still can’t believe it…the way it happened, that is,” Caden said, barely more than a whisper.

Mingo now spoke up. "Ya, and then Erik's sudden disappearance right after that." It seemed now that the flames were saying something to them. Not so much as words but thoughts and images, something nefarious and evil. Caden and Mingo looked at each other, half puzzled, half seeming to read each other's minds. It was that moment, it seemed, that all the questions they had were pointing to one ugly truth—Nadia's death wasn't a suicide, and somehow there was a connection to Erik's disappearance.

Kat and Nina didn't pick up on the exchange between Mingo and Caden. The thoughts of the women were focused more on missing Nadia and wishing she could have been there with them right now. Still, the flames continued to dance as if trying to tell a story.

Several minutes of somber silence passed, and finally Mingo broke the silence. He told the story of tribal legend and myth, of an evil spirit, which could possess a man because of evil deeds. The evil spirit, after taking possession of the man, would transform him into a great beast that could devour the flesh of innocent people and animals. The beast was called Wendigo and many other names in Indian legend.

The Wendigo, Mingo explained, stood some seven or eight feet tall on two hind legs. Kat said it sounded like the legend of Bigfoot, to which Mingo shook his head no. Mingo went on to describe the Wendigo as best as he could recall from boyhood stories. "It had a large wolf-like head with antlers like a great stag, gnashing teeth, and slashing claws. It is said that it had a muscular body with matted hair and glowing, demon-like eyes."

Mingo continued with what he knew of the Wendigo legend. "Sometimes, as the legend goes, the beast would prey on innocents. Sometimes, it would take revenge on a person who had offended it while it was in human form." Mingo went silent for a few minutes, lost in thought, and then continued, "Some of the legends told of the Wendigo being able to return to its original human form, and some legends told of the Wendigo being unable to return to human form and simple vanishing or hiding. I've never seen one, so I can't say for sure." Mingo smiled and then winked at Caden, who chuckled back.

Kat was on the edge of her seat now, completely terrified of the thoughts being conjured up by Mingo's descriptions. If Mingo was trying to get even with Kat for her earlier prank, he was doing a good job.

Mingo went on to explain that even though it was part of tribal lore, he had never actually seen the Wendigo in human or beast form, so he couldn't swear that it was, in fact, a truth or a myth. But given that all legends and myths have some basis of reality, he couldn't discount it, even now in the twenty-first century.

Kat now had eyes as big as a Yooper's frying pan, completely absorbed in Mingo's story. "Do you think it's possible for there to be one, a Wendigo, here in the Upper Peninsula?" Kat blurted out.

Mingo just shrugged his shoulders. "The legends come down from Canada, the Great Lakes region, and even out into the Dakotas. I guess it's possible—that is, if they are real."

Mingo went on to ask, "How many Bigfoots or mountain lions have you seen in the UP?" He paused as if waiting for an answer from Kat.

Kat answered, "Well, just because you haven't seen one it doesn't mean they don't exist."

Mingo was staring into the embers of the now dying fire as he said softly, "Exactly!"

Chapter 16

LOST MINE

Adventure Bound Scout leaders Randy Adams and Reggie Townsend hadn't made their daily check-in by cell phone, which was precoordinated to be every day at noon. US Forest Service Ranger Tony Lindeman was still at the scout base camp located at Craig Lake State Park. This was the fourth time Amanda Adams and Claire Peterson attempted contact. Nothing…again.

The scout group has spent the night at Summit Lake last night. They had planned on using the Summit Lake camp as their spike camp to search for the mine shaft that Rosalie McCormick wanted them to look for. Tony Lindeman had been up to Summit Lake, and he knew the cell phone service could be sketchy up there even on a good day.

"Maybe all their batteries are dead?" queried Lindeman to both Amanda and Claire.

Amanda answered, "Not likely." She explained that her husband, Randy Adams, had made sure the group was carrying four portable solar packs to recharge phone batteries…for the daily check-ins and for emergency.

Both Amanda and Claire knew that the check-ins could be late if there was no cell service in the location the scouts were standing. The backup plan was to attempt comms every third hour—3:00 p.m., 6:00 p.m., 9:00 p.m., etc.—until communications was established. If after twelve hours no communication was made, they would notify Lindeman, the forest ranger. If there was no communication after twenty-four hours, Lindeman and a couple other forest rangers would hike into their last known location, following the scouts' originally planned route. When the forest rangers went in, they would notify the Marquette Community Emergency Response Team (CERT). The CERT would in turn be on standby and track the movement of the forest rangers. It was a solid plan, and no one worried yet.

The Crystal Falls scout troop had left their spike camp on Summit Lake an hour after daylight. The group had plotted the suspected mine entrance to be about an hour from their campsite, assuming they moved at a decent pace. That was not the case, however, as it was already 1:00 p.m., and they were only halfway there. Randy Adams, one of the scout leaders, had attempted four times to call his wife with no success. They were obviously in a dead zone for cell service. As the group moved through some old-growth virgin timber, they suddenly came into and area thick with blown-down trees lying crisscrossed like a cruel game of life-size pickup sticks. To add to the obstacle course of blown-down old trees, new-growth vegetation was coming up thick as split pea soup. After that, there was another patch of old-growth timber and then another abatis of thick undergrowth and fallen trees.

Everyone in the group was sweating hard now, even in the cool fall air. Suddenly, the group found itself surrounded by towering cliffs. They seemed to be in a maze of towering walls, which didn't show up on their topographical maps.

"Weird," Reggie Townsend said out loud, looking at his map, then the cliffs, then his compass, and finally back at his map. "Check the GPS," he said to Randy. "Okay, guys, packs off and map check. We break here for lunch," Reggie said as he turned back to the scouts.

The scouts all took up seats on the ground in a loose circle, some spreading their map sheets out while looking at their compasses and then the surrounding terrain. Randy dug into his day pack, pulled out his GPS, powered it up, and then waited for it to connect on available satellites. He then pulled out a granola bar, unwrapped it, and took a bite and then a swig of water from his water bottle. Randy was looking around at the towering walls of hematite, granite, and limestone. Unusual rock formations, Randy thought to himself as he finally looked back at his GPS.

Reggie was digging his GPS out now. Randy smacked his GPS a couple times with his hand and double-checked to make sure it was on. Nothing. The GPS was on, all right, but it was reporting "no satellite signal." "Something's wrong on my GPS, check yours, Regg!" Randy called to Reggie, who was now watching his GPS power up. The GPS screen digits were spinning now, searching for a satellite signal…nothing, no sat signal.

"I barely have two satellites!" Regg called back to Randy, both looking at each other, puzzled.

"That's why we have a map and compass, dude!" Randy laughed.

Regg and Randy sat down side by side, watching the scouts looking at their maps and eating whatever lunch snacks they each brought. Sweat was steaming off most of them now that their day packs were off. It had been rough going so far, and the proof was in their sweat. "You know, we might end up spending the night up here," Randy said to Reggie.

"Yep, we don't want to have to go through that leg-breaker jungle of crap in the dark," Reggie replied.

Randy and Reggie spread their maps out side by side to compare while looking at the faint spot on the GPS where the mine shaft was supposed to be. "Something's off here," Randy finally said to Regg.

"Ya, I know what you mean. Do you think maybe Rosalie McCormick gave us the wrong location?" Reggie replied. "It's always possible, but she was positive even when we asked her to verify it three times, remember?"

Randy nodded his head slowly in agreement. "Ya, or maybe we got turned around and off track going through those two blowdowns?"

Randy traced a route with a small stick on his map while looking at the dot on the GPS and the rock walls towering before them. "If you look closely at the contour lines on the map, you can see it," Randy said, his eyes widening in surprise as he looked more suspiciously at the rock walls before them. "There should be a blind entrance into that rock right there," Randy said as he pointed to the seemingly impenetrable wall in front of them.

Reggie held the map close to his face now, looking at the map, then the rock face, and back to his map. "You would never see it in a hundred years unless you knew what you were looking for," Reggie said. "Even so, maybe the entrance is on top of that cliff and not from down here."

"Maybe," replied Randy, "but based on the information from Mrs. McCormick, it should be near the bottom of the cliff."

With that, Reggie said, "Let's see where the boys think we are, then we will saddle up and go find it."

Randy gave an affirmative nod, and then the two scout leaders began talking to the boys and having each one in turn show them their location on the map and give their reason why. After satisfactory answers from each scout, the troop hoisted up their collective day packs and started plodding, single file, toward the fortress rock wall before them.

"Well, this is supposed to be it," exclaimed Randy as the group stood in a small crowd at the base of a towering cliff that reached skyward several hundred feet. Curious and puzzled glances flashed around the scout troop.

"Where?" blurted out young Thomas Adams, who was Randy Adams' son.

"That's what we need to figure out." Reggie smiled. "According to Mrs. McCormick's notes, the opening to the mine should be right about around here," Reggie said as he pointed his index finger at the rock wall.

"Okay, here's the plan," Randy said. "I will take half the group, and we will search to the left."

Reggie then chimed in, "And I will take the other half, and we will search to the right." Reggie continued, "We will meet back here in one hour to exchange notes on what we found. From there, we will decide our next move."

Randy added, "Right! Also, be prepared to spend the night here, so ration your water, snacks, and any food you might have left." The troop then split up into two search parties. A white rag was tied off on a branch to mark their assembly point, and then they were off to find the mine shaft opening.

Randy Adams and his group of scouts traveled to the left, working their way along the base of the cliff. After about fifteen minutes, they were back in the tangle of toppled trees and thick undergrowth. They were still moving along the base of the cliff for another ten minutes when they came across what looked like a chimney climb cut horizontally in the rock wall and back in the direction they had just come from. If someone had been twenty feet away, they would never have seen the cut back in the rock wall. Standing fifty feet away from the cliff bottom, they could see the vegetation was so thick that it would have been near impossible to even see the cliff wall.

In the other direction, Reggie's group was working easily along the base of the cliff. After about five minutes, one of the boys, Sam Hubbell, pointed out the turkey vultures circling in the sky up ahead. Reggie looked, said, "Yep," and wondered what dead thing they would discover up ahead.

Back at the chimney climb, Randy tied one end of the Perlon climbing rope around his waist and started free-climbing the chimney cut. The chimney formation was all but invisible from the front of the rock-faced cliff. Thirty feet up and invisible from ground level, Randy lifted himself to a narrow ledge. Rock rose to his left and right, while above him, about another forty feet up, was a rock ceiling. Ahead and cutting up and somewhat parallel to the rock face, a maw in the rock exposed darkness. *Could this be the entrance?* Randy thought to himself. He then called down to the boys below, "I found something, a passageway it looks like. Give me some slack while I check it out."

Down below, Randy's group of scouts started talking excitedly and giving high fives. Randy moved through the narrow passage, which looked like it ended abruptly after about twenty feet. He was in far enough now that the light was poor. "Crap," he whispered out loud. He had left his flashlight in his day pack. He kept moving forward slowly into the dark, wanting to feel the end of the passage with his own hands. Suddenly, the passage opened up to the left, which seemed to go deeper into the bulk of the cliff. "This is it!"

Randy said out loud. He turned back to have the boys send up his pack with flashlight. He would verify it before having the boys come up to check it out too. Then they would send a couple scouts back to bring the rest of the group.

The young Adventure Bound Scout in Reggie's group, Sam Hubbell, was a bit of a bird buff. Sam knew that if vultures were circling, there would more than likely be something dead that was attracting them. Sam hustled ahead of the group, anxious to discover the death that the vultures already knew was there.

Poor Sam. In his excitement to see what the vultures were eyeing up for their next meal, he didn't expect to find the mangled human body at the base of the cliff. Sam thought he knew how he would react to finding someone dead; after all, he liked horror movies and had seen enough dead bodies on television and in video games. The smell is what hit Sam like a punch to the gut. Sam saw the brown, red, and orange material and started running to get to it first. He stopped dead when the smell hit him, turning his youthful face a sickly color of green. The next thing he knew, he was retching his guts out like there was no tomorrow. Good thing he had a light lunch.

Reggie held the rest of the boys back and had no problem getting Sam to move back far enough to avoid the smell. "Stay here," Reggie told the boys as he stepped forward slowly, looking left, right, ahead, and then up. The body was badly mangled. The skull was half-crushed, probably from impact on the rocks after falling off the cliff. The limbs and torso looked like animals had already started tearing the flesh away. It looked like this poor soul had been a hunter, dressed in brown canvas pants, a red flannel shirt, and an orange hunting vest—at least what was left of it. Reggie didn't see a weapon or drag marks. This looked like a hunting accident gone bad, really bad. Still, Reggie knew that staying away from the body was best. Authorities would still want to investigate, and their tracks all over the area would not be helpful. Reggie and the scouts visually scanned the area…there didn't seem to be anything else or any other bodies. Reggie tried calling base camp…still no signal.

Reggie recorded the grid coordinate of the body and hustled his group of scouts back to the linkup point marked with the white rag.

Two scouts from Randy's group were already there. The two groups excitedly exchanged news of the two discoveries—the body and the mine shaft.

It wasn't 6:00 p.m. yet, but Reggie tried to call base camp again. Amanda and Claire would still be waiting for contact from the scout group. Nothing, still no cell service. Reggie needed to get the group to Randy's location by the opening of the mine shaft to figure out their next move. It would be dark soon, and they would need to make camp at the base of the cliffs that night.

The news of finding the mine shaft opening was exciting. Finding the body was also exciting, in a morbid sense, but still important. Finding the body and mine shaft so close together left Reggie feeling uncomfortable. Reggie was beginning to get a bad feeling in his gut.

After the two groups were reunited by the chimney leading up to the mine shaft opening, they set about the task of setting up a primitive camp. Randy concurred with Reggie's gut feeling of something ominous. They would take precautions that night. Two were to be up at all times to tend to the fire and watch for any danger. The scout group was in survival mode now.

The light day packs they each carried only had the minim of the survival essentials. Still, the group took it all in stride. The weather had been good to them so far, and there was no indication of rain or bad weather for that night. This would be another memorable night around a campfire, speculating about the mine shaft, the dead body, and maybe even a ghost story or two. The young men still had a sense of being part of nature, but discovery of the mine shaft and the body certainly added a different twist to their sense of what nature was all about.

Chapter 17

ANOTHER DISAPPEARANCE

Caden, Nina, Kat, and Mingo just finished unpacking the black Toyota Tacoma and hauling bags and equipment back up to their apartments in Marquette. It had been a great getaway weekend at Jake and Susan Catrin's place. The group had butchered and packaged Nina and Kat's venison on Sunday. As it turned out, Caden and Mingo didn't shoot anything, but they still had a great time seeing and passing on several bucks.

They didn't have room in their apartment freezers for all the ground venison burger, steaks, roasts, and stew meat, so about half of it was left in the Catrins' large chest freezer to pick up as visits allowed. Nina and Kat gave half of the venison to Caden and Mino to keep in their freezer. Chances are they would be sharing meals as they usually did on the weekends.

The group had made it back to Marquette in time to make their Monday afternoon classes. After the unpacking and quick settling back into apartment life, all four were off in different directions heading out to their respective classes. They would give Troy and Sydney an update on their weekend when they all met for supper that evening at the main campus cafeteria.

Afternoon classes had passed quickly, and now it was back to campus cafeteria food for the week. The student meal package was a good deal, and it saved time and money. It only left the weekends to scavenge for meals on a student budget.

"Well, it sure isn't Mom's home cooking," Kat said as she picked at her grilled fish and vegetables.

"True, but at least it's a balanced meal on a student's schedule and budget," replied Caden.

"Always the practical one." Mingo laughed.

Caden, Nina, Mingo, and Kat were all seated in their usual place in the main student cafeteria for the evening meal. Travis and Sydney still hadn't shown up. "Probably just running late from a class or study group," Nina said, looking at the empty seats.

Everyone had almost finished eating when Mingo noticed Detectives Stannis Ryker and Pete Shelby from the Marquette police department standing near the main entrance to the cafeteria. The two detectives appeared to be scanning the room, as if looking for someone. When Ryker's eyes locked on the location Caden and his cohorts were sitting, both detectives headed toward Caden Garrett's group.

Caden stood and extended his hand to Ryker when the two detectives reached the table. Ryker hesitated a moment, looking at Shelby, then shook Caden's hand. Likewise, Caden shook Detective Shelby's hand, inviting the two detectives to sit down. Nods were exchanged between the students and the two detectives.

"Any word on Erik Thompson?" asked Caden.

"Actually, we were hoping to talk with your two friends, Troy Jackson and Sydney Willington," said Ryker without acknowledging Caden's question about Erik Thompson.

The gesture, or lack of response, didn't go unnoticed by the students as glances were exchanged. This obviously wasn't a friendly social call by the detectives.

"So what's going on, detectives? Obviously you still don't have jack shit on Erik's disappearance," Caden burrowed in. He didn't appreciate the accusatory stance the detectives seemed to be taking with them.

Ryker didn't like Caden Garrett's sudden disrespectful tone. The marine sergeant started coming out in him as he set aside his "hometown hero, friend of the students" demeanor. Ryker's brow started to furrow as if focusing to tackle a running back from his days of playing middle linebacker for Northern Michigan University fifteen years ago.

Caden Garret and the group could feel the tension mounting. Caden was cool under pressure, but he wasn't going to be bullied by this oversized cop who suddenly wanted to play mister tough guy with them—an obvious ploy to intimidate them.

Detectives Ryker and Shelby had already done background checks on all the members of this little oddball group. Ryker knew that Caden Garret and Mingan Grey Wolf had served in the army in some type of Special Operations unit and that both had honorable discharges with a lot of distinctive combat service. It didn't matter; Ryker had heard of lots of these "special operator" types going rouge. He needed to put pressure on them and get something to break loose.

Ryker had gotten another one of his boss' famous ass chewing again that morning for still having a big fat *zero* on the scoreboard for leads to finding Erik Thompson. To make things worse, another student was reported as missing. Ryker was not having a good day and he would be damned if this punk college kid would make it any worse.

"All these kids are clean, Ryker, no record, not even a parking ticket between them," Shelby said, trying to defuse things a little. Shelby knew Ryker was trying to put pressure on these students, scare them a little, but Ryker was quickly heading over the line. With Caden Garrett's sudden pushing back, Shelby saw the situation going nowhere but bad…real quick.

"How about getting us a couple cups of coffee, Stannis. I'll buy," Shelby said to Ryker as he shoved a five-dollar bill in his hand and stood between him and the table where the students were sitting. Ryker glared at Caden Garret as the detective slowly took the bill and headed to the coffee machines. It was a "this isn't over" glare, and Caden knew it.

"Sorry about that, we've been having a rough couple of days," said Shelby as he sat down, adapting a more sociable and friendly demeanor. "Another student has been reported as missing," Shelby started. "She, Mary Stueben, was last seen with Troy Jackson, Sydney Willington, and some other students Saturday night at the Wooden Nickel downtown Marquette."

The Wooden Nickel was a popular college hangout in the evenings for a bite to eat, a drink, or some dancing. It wasn't a big place but it was oftentimes packed with college students letting loose on Friday and Saturday nights.

Looks of concern suddenly flashed around the table. Troy and Syd still hadn't shown up for their evening group ritual of supper together. They were now over an hour late.

Shelby continued, "We were hoping to talk with Troy and Sydney to maybe find out when they last saw Mary Stueben or where they went after the Wooden Nickel." Shelby picked up the sudden change in the mood of the group, from interested to concerned. Ryker, just returning with two cups of coffee, picked up on the flash of concern around the group too. He decided to keep his mouth shut and watch to see where Shelby's questions were going.

Nina and Kat explained to Shelby that they were waiting for Troy and Sydney right now and that they should have been there by now. Kat also told how they—Caden, Nina, Mingo, and herself—had left town Friday and spent the weekend at her parents' place near Manistique hunting. She gave the detectives Jake and Susan Catlin's phone number to verify her story.

Caden was already calling Troy on his cell phone while Mingo texted Sydney. Nothing. No answer. No reply to the text. "Nothing," explained Caden as he looked up at the group and then to the two detectives. "Troy and Sydney aren't answering!"

The mood of the group suddenly turned dark. "Tell us what you know, maybe we can help," Caden offered to Shelby. Caden was intentionally ignoring Ryker.

"This is a police matter, we will handle it," said Ryker firmly.

"Really," said Caden, determined. "You still don't have any leads on Erik's disappearance. Another student is missing. Two more of our friends could be missing. That on top of the death of a friend, which was ruled as a suicide that, quite frankly, I seriously doubt was an actual suicide." Caden was verbally sticking his finger into Ryker's chest.

The last part of Caden Garrett's comment struck Ryker like getting shot with a harpoon. "A suicide that I seriously doubt was an actual suicide. What makes you say that?" asked Ryker. It's not that Ryker didn't have the same thoughts; he just found it peculiar coming from Caden Garrett, especially now. Maybe Garrett and his friends knew more than they were saying.

"Think about it, there was nothing going on with Nadia's life that would even give the slightest hint of suicide," said Caden. "It still doesn't make any sense to us," Caden continued. "Look, these are our friends. Like it or not, we are vested in finding answers. Based on what you have so far, it seems to me that you can use all the help you can get," said Caden, making his case for being included in the investigation. It was more of a conciliatory statement rather than accusatory. But that's not how detective Ryker took it.

"You can't be involved in an official investigation, period," said Ryker defiantly. "We have the badges, you don't. As far as we are concerned, we still don't know for sure that you didn't have anything to do with these disappearances…and death," Ryker said, determined and looking straight at Caden on the word *death*.

Everyone in the group looked astonished at Ryker as he made his last statement. It even caught Detective Shelby off guard. Ryker felt the need to push on Garrett.

"Are you fucking kidding?" was Caden's response to Ryker.

"Don't use that tone of voice with me, boy!" Ryker growled.

"Do your fucking job and I won't have to," Caden growled back.

Things were looking to get out of hand real quick. Caden was getting ready to deal hurt and destruction; Mingo had seen it many times when they were in combat. For Caden, badge or no badge, there was something going on with Ryker that Caden could feel was off, something very wrong. It was more of a gut feeling than anything, but it was there. Caden wasn't going to be backed down by his bullshit bully tactics.

Shelby grabbed Ryker by the arm, stopping the big man from grabbing Caden Garrett.

Mingo stepped in between Caden and Ryker, more to stop Caden from moving into action rather than to protect him.

"I think we're done for now," said Detective Shelby. "When you see your friends, tell them we need to talk to them. Meet me here tomorrow, same time," finished Shelby as he led Ryker away from the group.

"What the hell was that, Caden?" Nina said, looking at Caden and then at the group, referring to Ryker's whole change in demeanor. "I know they were using 'good cop, bad cop' with us, but to insinuate we are suspects? That's a little too much, don't you think?" Caden replied.

Mingo spoke up. "Think about it from their perspective. They are groveling for leads and have nothing. They are getting pressure from the press and their highers. And the only thing they see as a common factor is our group."

"I don't know Mary Stueben, do any of you?" There were shaking heads around the group...no one knew her.

"What about Troy or Sydney?" said Kat. "Maybe they had a class or study group with her."

"Maybe...probably," said Caden reluctantly. "Nina and Kat, how about checking with Syd's apartment and roommate? Mingo and I will go check Troy's apartment and talk to his roomies. We can meet back at our apartment when we are done."

An hour later, the four met at Caden and Mingo's apartment. They were beginning to feel like the Marquette detectives with a big zero on their scoreboard. Sydney's roommate hadn't seen Syd since Saturday evening, about 8:00 p.m., when she took off to meet Troy at the Wooden Nickel.

It was a similar story when Caden and Mingo talked to Troy's roommates. Troy had left about 8:00 p.m. for the Wooden Nickel to meet up with Sydney, and he still had not returned. Something was definitely wrong here. Neither Troy nor Syd had been seen since Saturday night.

Chapter 18

CAUGHT IN THE ACT

Little Tony was one of those huge unassuming guys who had a roaring laugh and hands so big he could spike your head into a basketball hoop, along with the rest of your body. He was also a part-time bouncer at the Wooden Nickel and Vera Bar, two popular weekend hangouts for the college students in Marquette. Caden knew Tony from his mixed martial arts workouts and from the gym where they would occasionally lift weights together. Tony Braddock, or Little Tony, had played football for NMU and graduated several years ago. He could have gone on to play professional football but found himself on the wrong end of the law at the end of his senior year. The two-year jail stint cancelled his contract with the New York Giants. For a big guy, Tony was fast and agile. In a fight, Tony would be the guy you wanted in your corner. Caden went up against Tony in a few martial arts workouts and knew that Tony was a very capable fighter. Tony could crush a man if he got a hold of you, something Caden avoided in his one-on-one match-ups. Caden considered Little Tony a friend, but he really didn't know Tony that well, so it was more of a "workout buddy" relationship built on mutual respect.

"Hey, Tony!" Caden half-shouted as he made his way into the Wooden Nickel. Tony was perched in the bouncer's stool watching the customers. Then he saw Caden and put on his big friendly smile, said, "Hey Dude!" and gave Caden a high five and a fist bump.

"How you been, man?" Caden asked as he glanced over the boisterous crowd of students in the bar area.

"Good…in fact, great!" Tony said with a hint of excitement in his booming voice. "A rep from the WWE contacted me and asked if I was interested in getting on the local circuit with a couple televised bouts in Wisconsin and Michigan this winter. They said it would be as an opponent to a couple of the big-name stars, but it could get me in big-time if things work out. Then I got a call from the security guys up at the Huron Mountain Club. Apparently, they are forming a security business owned by Huron Mountain Club to work security jobs in the area. They want to start me out as one of their security team leaders, with promotion potential beyond that."

"That's great, Tony! Which one are you thinking about taking?" asked Caden.

"I don't know yet. I might actually get to work both opportunities," replied Toni.

"I'm happy for you, Tony. It sounds like things are really starting to happen for you," said Caden, expressing approval.

Tony smiled back. "Hey, I still have a bouncer job for when you're ready!"

Caden slapped Tony on the shoulder. "I couldn't afford the liability if I hurt someone."

"That's why we have liability insurance, dude!" Tony laughed back.

"Tony, on a more serious note, I need to ask you something," Caden said as he produced photos of Troy Jackson and Sydney Willington. "Do you remember seeing these two friends of mine here last Saturday night?"

"You know, that asshole detective, Ryker, asked me the same thing," explained Little Tony. "I didn't tell him shit." Tony's mood had suddenly turned dark and angry. Obviously, Tony Braddock didn't care much for Detective Stannis Ryker.

"Whoa! I would have thought you two would be tight, seeing as both of you played ball for NMU," Caden said with surprise at Tony's reaction.

"He is the reason I spent two years in the slammer, man," explained Tony. "The guy set me up to take a fall for some bullshit I had nothing to do with," continued Tony.

"You're joking, right?" asked Caden in disbelief of what he was hearing from Tony.

"I'm not kidding, dude, I think he set me up to protect someone else. That sorry piece of shit can kiss my ass if he ever wants anything from me…other than a throat punch or elbow to the face." Tony wasn't saying anything positive about Ryker, that was for sure. Definitely bad blood there.

"I was under the impression he was a good cop and well liked by the Marquette community, students, and staff at NMU?" said Caden. "Ya, he's got a lot of people fooled, including you, it looks like," Tony replied.

"Sorry, man," Caden said. "I had no idea about him setting you up like that."

"No problem. Karma has a way of catching up with dipshits like that," said Tony. "As to your friends, yes, they were here Saturday night, hanging with a group of other students…it looked like it, anyway."

"Can you tell me anything about them, the other students?" Caden asked Tony.

Just then, Nina worked her way in through the doors of the Wooden Nickel. "Hey, babe!" Caden said as Nina moved over to Caden's side. "Tony, you remember my girlfriend Nina?" said Caden to Tony.

"Hard to forget a woman this good-looking," Tony said with a big smile as he took Nina's hand in a big mitt. "I'm really sorry to hear about your cousin Nadia, Nina," Tony said with sincere empathy.

Nina smiled back. "Thanks, Tony, I still find it hard to believe she's gone sometimes."

It happened almost midsentence as Nina was talking, Tony's face turned from condolence to surprise, as if a light bulb suddenly lit up. Both Caden and Nina saw it at the same time. "What?" they both said simultaneously.

"Caden, Erik, and Nadia were hanging with some of the same people that Troy and Sydney were with last Saturday night! I should have realized it before now," said Tony, his eyes going from sudden surprise to almost subdued.

Caden and Nina looked at each other with both surprise and bewilderment.

"Are you sure, Tony?" asked Caden.

"Yes," Tony replied, "because one of them was the guy who offered me the security position up at Huron Mountain... Dirk Astor. He and his buddies started coming here on weekends after classes started. I think Astor and his pals go to Michigan Tech, but they belong to the Huron Mountain Club. Lots of money there, I'll tell you. Real party animals, buying drinks for everyone, schmoozing the local chicks, friendly with everyone. They seemed harmless, really, just having a good time."

"Tony," Caden said with all the seriousness he could muster, "Troy and Sydney haven't been seen since Saturday night here at the Wooden Nickle."

Caden and Nina were beginning to understand the sudden flex in Tony's expressions. "Don't worry, Tony. If there is nothing to this, we won't compromise you with the Huron Mountain Club. The fact of the matter is, however, we may need your help."

"Shit!" Tony murmured to himself. He didn't like this sudden potential turn in his luck, but he reluctantly agreed to help Caden and Nina if he could.

There were dots that were starting to connect, and somehow Tony was being drawn in, just like the last time he was set up. Tony trusted Caden and had no problem helping him; it was the long arm of the law, specifically the Stannis Ryker part of this whole thing, which gave Tony the uneasy feeling.

Caden and Nina waded their way through the gathering crowd to the table where Mingo and Kat had already staked a claim. For a Friday night, the Wooden Nickel had started packing people in early; they were lucky to get the table. Soon there would be a waiting line outside as the establishment reached capacity.

"Well, I think the buckless Yoopers should be buying tonight," proclaimed Kat as Caden and Nina took seats at the table. Nina chuckled and agreed.

Caden and Mingo looked at each other with devious smiles, and Mingo said, "I'll get the first round." It seemed that Kat was well past *her* first round. She was celebrating an *A* she got on a test for her toughest class.

Nina and Caden filled Mingo and Kat in on what Tony, the bouncer, had told them about the same people being with Erik and Nadia, as were with Troy and Sydney before they disappeared.

"Maybe we should tell Ryker and Shelby," Mingo finally said after Caden and Nina finished.

"Maybe," said Caden, "but Tony doesn't trust Ryker. In fact, Little Tony said that Ryker set him up for the time he spent in prison."

"What!" exclaimed Mingo. "No way!"

"That's exactly what I thought," replied Caden, "but given the way Ryker was acting the last time we talked and the hunch I have that there might be something to Tony's story, maybe we should wait until we know a couple things for sure first."

"What do you have in mind...and what things are you talking about?" Nina said to Caden.

"Well, based on what Tony said, this Dirk Astor guy has something to do with the Huron Mountain Club and was seen with both Erik and Nadia and Troy and Sydney before they disappeared. Maybe we should just come right out and ask Astor what happened." Caden continued, "Quite frankly, I'm surprised that Ryker hadn't figured this much out yet."

"Maybe he did and he's just not saying anything to us," Kat said.

"Ya, I mean it's not like you and Ryker are getting nominated as buddies of the year." Nina scoffed. That brought chuckles around the table just as a waitress brought four beers and four shots of Hot Damn.

"Ah, troublemakers tonight, I see," Kat said as she eyed her two drinks. Mingo smiled slyly as he paid and tipped the waitress. Yes, the waitress with all the curves in the right places and a seductive smile aimed right at Mingo. Mingo couldn't help but blush and return the smile with as manly a smile as he could muster.

Caden saw it and laughed. Mingo blushed again and cursed at Caden under his breath.

Mingo was a guy you wanted on your side when you got in a tough spot. When it came to Mingo and women, though, well, he was on the shy side, unless you knew him, of course. Even then, he was usually a man of few words, and even fewer when it came to talking to the opposite sex.

Nina tried to bail Mingo out of his embarrassment by raising her shot glass and saying, "To the buckless Yoopers!"

Kat laughed and then blurted out, "Hear, hear...to the buckless Yoopers!" Caden and Mingo tapped their shot glasses on the table, said in unison, "Whatever!" and downed their shots in synchronization as if it had been well rehearsed.

The waitress with all the right curves in all the right places was passing by their table again on her way back to the bar to fill another order and stopped behind Mingo. "We need another one?" she said, pressing up against Mingo so he could feel her heat and the presence of one of her amazing and firm breasts just touching his head. This gal knew how to work for tips.

"Sure, another round of shots, same thing," said Caden, smiling at Mingo and raising his eyebrows in a knowing manner. Mingo was starting to find his courage and ask Miss Curvy what her name was, but just as he turned, she was off to the bar to fill the order.

"Stop it," Nina said to Caden.

"I think she likes Mingo," Caden said back.

"Well, he is a good-looking guy," said Kat. "What's there to not like about Mingo?" This time, she was looking at Mingo with flirting eyes.

"All right you guys, what is this, 'let's get Mingo a date' night?" said Mingo, half-frustrated, half-humorous. They all laughed.

"I don't think we are going to have to do anything. I think she might be dragging you out back by the hair to have her way with you if you keep putting on the Mr. Innocent act." Caden laughed.

"No, she's just trying to provide good service and get a good tip," countered Mingo.

"Okay, so that's your story and you're sticking to it?" Caden said, countering Mingo's counter.

The table bantered back and forth in good fun with the curvy waitress contributing to the momentum by flirting more and more with Mingo. Finally, to Mingo's relief, Crystal—the curvy waitress—

gave Mingo her phone number and told him to call her. But first, she wanted him to come out to Big Bon's tomorrow night so see her dance.

Big Bon's was the only gentlemen's club in the Upper Peninsula and about thirty minutes from Marquette off Highway 35 near the town of Rock.

"It looks like she wants to take away the Mr. Shy Mingo and make a man out of you," Caden chided. Mingo clearly didn't see the humor in it.

"Ya, me and every other guy in the place," Mingo said.

Kat was looking up at the bar and a new group that had worked their way into the Wooden Nickel. "Excuse me," Kat said, "I'm going to go over and introduce myself to Mr. Hottie up at the bar." Kat got up, put on her sexiest walk, and slinked up to the bar, just one stool down from Mr. Hottie.

Caden was almost shocked, but he figured girls just gotta have fun too. Caden could see Kat was getting drunk, but he assessed she was still in control and wouldn't do anything too regrettable. Kat was still his little cousin and "little sister," whom he would have to watch out for and which he planned on doing.

It only took Kat a couple minutes and she had Mr. Hottie's undivided attention.

Another couple, whom Caden didn't know, asked to sit down at their table. Now that Kat was up and away from their table, there were three empty chairs. The new couple sat down but mostly talked between themselves.

The Wooden Nickel was really hopping now. Everyone was talking loudly, the music was up loud, and there were couples now up dancing on the dance floor. It was a typical campus bar on a weekend night—young people growing up, playing the mating game, and killing brain cells.

Caden was now talking with Nina, keeping one eye on cousin Kat, who was still making points with Mr. Hottie up at the bar. Mingo was people-watching, enjoying the music, and eye-stalking Crystal, the waitress with all the curves in the right places. It was hard not to watch her. She was pretty, sexy, and a big hit with most of the guy customers, not to mention curves in all the right places—ya… worth repeating.

Caden watched as Kat excused herself from the bar and went over to the women's restroom. It was subtle, but Caden picked up on it, as did Mingo. Mr. Hottie did a slight head nod to Crystal, who dog-tailed over to him while ignoring several other customers. She stepped close to him, as if speaking in confidence, for a brief verbal exchange. Their manner seemed to be familiar but businesslike. Very subtly, she nodded at their table, whereas then Mr. Hottie looked at them as if to size them up.

Caden and Mingo both saw the look but pretended not to notice. The hair on Caden' back was up now. He didn't like the looks of this one bit.

Kat was coming out of the bathroom now, her makeup freshened up and her front buttons taken down a couple notches so that she was showing her sexiest self.

Caden had seen about as much as he wanted of Mr. Hottie and was about to go get Kat and haul her back to their table. Just as Caden was about to stand, Crystal, in all her curvy glory, appeared with another round of drinks. "Compliments of Mr. Smith at the bar," Crystal said, beaming perfect white teeth and good looks that could make a good man bad.

Mingo, Nina, and Caden looked toward the bar, and there Mr. Hottie and Kat were raising a shot glass in their direction. "Maybe this guy isn't so bad," said Mingo.

"The jury is still out," Caden replied, the hair on his back still standing on end.

"Let me go invite him to sit with us," said Nina.

"Okay, that way we can keep a better eye on Kat to make sure she doesn't get into trouble," Caden replied. Nina looked back at Caden. "I think Kat can probably take care of herself."

Nina got up, walked up to the bar, and sidled up alongside Kat. "Hi, I'm Nina. Would you like to join us at our table?" she said to Mr. Hottie. Nina could see that he was extremely good-looking with a good build and, when he smiled, extremely charismatic and disarming. She automatically liked the guy but felt like something was off.

"I'm John Smith," he said, flashing his GQ smile and "innocent boy" looks at Nina.

Kat was swaying ever so slightly. "See?" she said. "Mr. Hottie."

John Smith laughed. "Kat, you are hilarious. I don't want you to like me for my good looks and body. I have a lot of money and a pleasant personality too!" Both Nina and Kat laughed.

Another round of shots was served up to Nina and Kat before they stopped laughing. "To new friends!" announced John Smith. And with that, he had the girls completely disarmed, clinking shot glasses and going bottoms up.

It seemed now that the original group John Smith was with was pressing in around the two women, laughing and talking loud. Then John Smith grabbed Kat by the hand and said, "Let's dance, this is one of my favorite songs!" Kat followed, giggling as she went; she loved dancing.

Caden and Mingo couldn't see either Nina or Kat now. The group of Mr. Hottie's friends had somehow shifted to block their view. At first, it seemed like the natural flow of bodies moving around in a crowded bar and dance floor. Mingo saw Kat heading out on the dance floor, holding the hand of Mr. GQ from the bar. He almost expected to see Nina following behind with another guy. "I see Kat on the dance floor," said Mingo, "but I can't see Nina." Caden sat still, watching more closely.

Nina felt a hand squeezing her butt. She knew Caden should be here right now, but she felt so good, so erotic, and so horny. She moved away, but the hand kept hold of her, and another hand was on her breast. The group seemed to be squeezing in closer now, more hands, someone trying to grab between her legs.

"We are glad to see you decided to dump those two losers," said a voice coming from the guy that was now holding Nina from behind, hands on her breasts, and inhaling deeply on the back of her neck.

Meanwhile, out on the dance floor, Mr. GQ had started making out with Kat, creating quite the spectacle of grabbing her ass while

Kat wrapped herself tight to Mr. Hottie, John Smith. Kat felt sex crazed now as Mr. Hottie groped her and worked his tongue in her mouth. Kat had never felt this horny in all her life, and she didn't care what she looked like.

Caden and Mingo were trying to get up, but they felt like something or someone was holding them down with all their weight. "They spiked the drinks!" Caden said to Mingo. Mingo had already realized it, too, and was having his own issues trying to fight his way to his feet. Two guys were standing behind them pressing down on their shoulders, preventing them from getting up.

Caden and Mingo were finally on their feet, and the two fellows whose job it was to keep them down were now lying on the floor unconscious. A reverse arm wrap and back fist to Caden's man did the trick. Mingo opted for a less subtle approach by heeling his chair into his man's groin and aiming a straight down punch to the man's head.

It was then that the big shadow came. It was Tony. He had been busy with the crowd outside and come back in just in time to see what was going on. Dirk Astor and his friends had been let in through the workers' door in the back.

"Hey, Caden, that's Dirk Astor out there doing the nasty with your cousin Kat!"

Caden looked at Tony, barely able to move. "They spiked our drinks, Tony. Get the girls out of there!"

Tony knew his job at Huron Mountain would all but vanish if he confronted Dirk Astor. Tony was getting a clear picture of what was happening, and Kat and Nina would be the next to disappear if he didn't do something quick. Tony grabbed the nearest co-bouncer and told him to get Kat and take her to the office when he pulled the fire alarm.

The fire alarm screamed as patrons were flooding out the front doors and exits of the Wooden Nickel. Sam Tuttle, another bouncer at the Wooden Nickel, got Kat and pulled her to the manager's office.

Tony Braddock caught up with Dirk Astor's group as they were making their way out the back emergency exit with Nina. Tony was able to push bodies out the exit and shield Nina from being taken with them. After the door was clear, Tony took Nina to the manager's office and told her to go inside and wait.

Caden and Mingo followed out the back emergency exit to the rear parking lot. There Dirk Astor was bitching out his group of silver-spooned cronies for letting their *prize* get away.

"You lost yours too," a big, tough-looking guy said to Dirk. Dirk was facing away from the emergency exit when Caden approached him from the rear. Caden had picked up a table leg from a broken table lying by the back door. Caden swung the old table leg as hard as his paralyzed body would allow, striking Dirk Astor alongside the head and knocking him out cold. Mingo had grabbed a broom handle and jammed it in the sternum of the closest goon who thought this would be an easy fight. The guy was on the ground, unable to breathe.

Within seconds, Caden and Mingo had whittled down the odds from ten in Astor's pack to eight. The odds still weren't good enough in their stupefied and drugged condition. Caden and Mingo had faced tougher odds in worse conditions, so they would not be deterred.

Astor's group now gang-charged Caden and Mingo. The first two of the pack went down quickly, Mingo making a wide swinging arch with the broom handle to smack a temple and Caden coming down hard with his table leg striking another square between the eyes.

There were six remaining, but they weren't deterred by their colleagues going down on the ground in groans and yells of pain and agony. Caden was choking out his next victim, while three more piled on, punching and kicking Caden wherever they could find an opening. In retrospect, Caden would later remember, probably not the best move for trying to even up the odds when outnumbered, six to two, and being drugged.

Mingo had kneecapped one guy with a side-thrust kick, putting him down and out of the fight. The next guy tackled Mingo, taking the fight to the ground. The drugs were just too powerful, and in the end, Caden and Mingo couldn't muster the strength, speed, and agility to beat these guys or put up a winning fight. They never saw the big goon dragging Kat from around the front of the building and tossing her into one of Astor's vehicles.

By the time the fire trucks and the police showed up, Astor and his crew of predators had gone. Caden had managed to choke out the guy he was working over but not without taking a beating to the head and body by the three other guys. Mingo had managed to put one more guy out of the fight, eye-gouging him and twisting his testicles into a square knot. Still, Mingo had gotten pretty beat up too. It was hard doing offense and defense while moving in slow motion.

Detective Ryker and Shelby had talked to Caden and Mingo before releasing them. "It's punks like you who give towns like this a bad reputation," Ryker said pointedly at Caden. "If you know what's good for you, you will take your sorry ass to some Podunk community college and leave Marquette."

Ryker finished his college pep talk by telling the two to get the get the fuck out of his sight before he had them arrested for public intoxication.

Caden was still too sluggish from being drugged to put up an argument. One thing was for sure, though—Ryker was starting to piss Caden off. Not only did this asshole Astor get off scot-free, but Ryker didn't even want to hear about it. As soon as Caden brought up Dirk Astor's name, Ryker was done listening.

Caden and Mingo went back into the Wooden Nickel and into the manager's office where Nina was sitting quietly waiting for them. Nina started crying and hugged Caden. Kat wasn't there.

Tony now entered the manager's office and looked around the group at the circle of dismal faces. He explained that Caden and Mingo had been drugged with some type of tranquilizer and that Nina's and Kat's drinks had been laced with ecstasy and a sedative. He then explained how he had managed to save Nina from Dirk Astor and that he had sent one of the other bouncers to get Kat and bring her to the office as well. A questioning look suddenly took over Tony's face as he looked at Nina.

"Where is Kat?" Tony exclaimed.

To everyone's horror, Nina replied, "Kat wasn't here!"

Tony looked back at Caden. "Shit!" they both said in unison.

No one was in any condition to continue the fight, nonetheless drive to pursue the Astor gang of thugs. Tony was finally able to convince the group that their next stop should be the campus medical clinic. From there they could file police reports and regroup for their next action.

The four took a taxi to the hospital extension clinic on campus to get blood drawn to determine what they had been drugged with. They also contacted the campus police department to report the sexual assault incident; they wanted it documented.

Unfortunately, because the initial incident took place off campus, the campus cops turned the matter over to the Marquette police department. When two officers showed up to take statements, it was none other than Detectives Ryker and Shelby. As best they could, Caden and Mingo tried to get the two cops to understand that Dirk Astor had taken Kat. Shelby pretended to take notes, but Ryker just watched Caden with distain.

Finally, Ryker asked them all, "Did you actually see Dirk Astor take Kat?"

No, unfortunately none of them saw Astor take her but then pleaded with Ryker that they knew he did as they tried to explain.

"I'm sorry," Shelby finally said. There is nothing we can do if no one saw him take her. Quite frankly, it would just be your word against theirs."

Then, as if to add final insult to injury, Ryker said, "And I, for one, would be more inclined to take Astor's word over yours," looking pointedly at Caden again.

Caden was right about at boiling point with this asswipe Ryker. Caden focused and held back. He knew Ryker was trying to set him up. Yeah, knock out this asshole cop and get locked up. That's right where Ryker would want him—sitting in jail, unable to do anything to save Kat, messing up his college plans, and basically screwing his life over with a felony charge and conviction. Just like he had done to Tony.

Mingo read Ryker's intent and maintained self-control. Ryker was going for the *setup* to get both of them thrown in jail and basically hamstrung in doing anything about going after Dirk Astor and getting Kat back.

The one thing Caden and Mingo knew for sure at this moment was to not get baited into Ryker's trap. They both knew that nothing would come of Ryker and Shelby's report and that it would only get lost somewhere or get submitted as just some college kids doing drugs.

This deadly game Caden and Mingo found themselves snagged in was going to call for some strategic thinking and fast.

Chapter 19

CHALLENGE

Jake Catrin, Kat's father, could feel his blood boiling as he loaded up his SUV with gear. Caden had called him an hour ago to fill him in on the sexual assault, the drugging, the fight, Kat being taken, and the law's deaf ear. Caden had been more concerned about Kat and Nina than himself and Mingo. Caden had told Jake that this Asher guy and his goons were probably behind Troy and Sydney's disappearance and possibly even behind Erik's disappearance and Nadia's suicide. Bottom line, this kidnapping wasn't going to get covered up by dirty cops, and Caden would need Jake's help to find out what happened to Troy and Sydney.

Caden and Mingo were getting ready for action now. They knew that they would need to get into the secretive Huron Mountain Club grounds to get at Astor and to find Kat, Troy, Sydney, and Erik…if they were still alive. This wasn't going to be easy.

The last thing Dirk Astor said to them as he was gaining consciousness and being dragged off to one of the silver Mercedes Rovers was that when Dirk saw them again, he was going to kill them. It didn't sound like an idle threat, and Mingo told them, "Not if we see you first." This was a challenge to the death, and Caden and Mingo knew it. This was another "kill or be killed" scenario. Dirk Astor had started this, laid down the death challenge, and now Caden and Mingo were going to finish it.

Chapter 20

COUNTER CHALLENGE

One of Dirk Astor's *boys* was at the wheel of one of the silver Mercedes, which was followed closely by the black Cadillac Escalade as they raced by the guard shack leading into the prestigious and secretive grounds of the Huron Mountain Club.

"Give me a cell phone," Dirk Astor demanded. "I need to call my dad in New York and have him send in reinforcements and a cleanup party."

This wasn't the first time Dirk had to call in backup and a cleanup party. A few weeks back, one of Dirk's goons had killed some Indian chick they had drugged and brought back to the HMC for some "extracurricular recreation." Things had gotten out of hand, as they sometimes do, and big Tank Summerville had broken the girl's neck when she tried to get away. Tank was sent back to New York shortly after that to work on another one of Mr. Astor's "projects."

The last time the cleanup crew came in, they took the Indian girl's lifeless body back to her house in Marquette and staged the death to look like a suicide by hanging. It also involved the usual pay-offs to the Marquette medical examiner and visit to the Marquette police department. It's amazing what a group of professionals and a little money can accomplish.

The guy that had been with the Indian girl was tracked down and found still in a stupefied condition. The cleanup crew then drugged him again, dressed him up as if he had been hunting, and dumped him in the middle of the McCormick Wilderness area. He was injured just enough to never find his way out alive.

It was the typical cleanup job for these professionals who were used to cleaning up for a big-city mob *hit* or subcontracted hit for some unscrupulous political operatives in Washington, DC. It was no big deal; it was all in a day's work for these guys.

Dirk Astor didn't have any bodies yet that needed to be cleaned up, but he would—that is, after he killed the two Yooper rednecks and the couple that were chained up in an abandoned cabin.

Dirk Astor got off the cell phone with his dad. "They are sending out twenty guys and a cleanup crew," Dirk smirked. "I don't know who those assholes were, but they are going to be dead assholes when I'm done with them. It also looks like I will be changing universities again." Dirk laughed. "I won't be staying in this Podunk redneck hole in wall much longer…it looks like." Dirk looked at his car mate. "As soon as we finish up with the local yokels, that is." He spoke with venom practically dripping from his expression.

Chapter 21

CAVES OF DOOM

Adventure Bound Scout leader Randy Adams was in the lead with a makeshift torch and a small head-mounted LED light, which bounced and reflected off the mine shaft tunnel walls. His co-scout leader, Reggie Townsend, was bringing up the rear of the single-file trail of scouts. Each scout had one of the small head-mounted LED lights as they worked their way, lights flashing this way and that. From the line of boys came excited expressions of "Wow," "Look at this," or "Check this out." Reggie was carrying the only other makeshift torch for their troop, its dancing flames casting curious shadows against the craggy rock walls. Two boys were carrying unlit backup torches for when the first two would go out.

The previous night had gone by slowly as most of the troop was restless. They had slept on mats of leaves and branches with only a space blanket to keep warm. They had rotated fireguard in pairs all night, but truth be told, half the troop was up at any given time, keeping warm and dozing off by the fire.

Cell phone calls were attempted every three hours per their plan, but it was no use; the whole area seemed to be one large dead zone for reception. Randy and Reggie had discussed their options by the fire last night. Either they could head back to the last point of cell reception, thus attempting to make contact again, or they could explore the mine while they were still there. It had been agreed that the group would not split up again, at least not yet. They were already twenty-four hours past last contact, and they knew that forest rangers would be on their way soon. They figured they could be back in cell phone contact at Summit Lake within about six hours of daylight travel. That would also be a good point to link up with the forest rangers and guide them into where they had discovered the body.

The discovery of the mine shaft and the possibility of exploring the mine was almost too good an opportunity for the scout troop to pass up. They would have the time to explore for about half a day. Then they would have to head back to Summit Lake to contact Amanda and Claire at base camp, and thus notifying the forest rangers who should be on their way. If the mine shaft looked unsafe or too dangerous, they would end the exploring and head back to Summit Lake sooner. It seemed like a good plan.

The torch flames flickered and danced on the rock walls as the group moved slowly forward. Back at the base of the cliff, where the hidden chimney cut into the cliff face, they had left a fluorescent orange marker panel. If someone was looking for them, the way into the shaft could be easily discovered. One of their Perlon climbing ropes still dangled down the jagged stone in the chimney climb and was anchored at the top on the entry ledge. On their return, it would be a short rappel down from the ledge to the bottom of the cliff.

The first twenty feet in from the ledge was a natural cut or break in the rock cliff. Where the shaft actually started was as the opening broke off to the left at the end of the first cave. Markings on the wall indicated that the shaft into the bulk of the cliff formation had been widened with tools.

On the shaft floor, there was an old rusted-out metal mining lantern, from maybe the late 1800s or early 1900s, which indicated some presence in the shaft during the beginning of the UP mining rush. Etched into the stone near the first cutback were worn-down markings, which were difficult to make out. At the first left turn leading into the bulk of the great rock were more markings, some primitive, etched into the rock in sticklike characters. Neither Randy nor Reggie knew what the characters meant or said, but they figured they were ancient Indian or tribal markings. Some markings in faded colored strokes were slightly easy to decipher—a tree, a deer, a wolf, and a group of people. After another twenty feet, there was another faded colored picture. This one was much more curious. It looked like a battle between a group of people and a large animal, almost like a large antlered deer standing on two legs. It was tough to make out clearly, but it was interesting to see. The scouts were taking pictures as they went, excited to be documenting a truly unexpected find on their expedition. One of the boys exclaimed, "We're going to be in National Geographic!" Randy and Regg smiled at each other; they could feel the boyish excitement of these ancient discoveries too.

After about a hundred feet, from the first left turn, the shaft split into two different tunnels. The tunnel angling to the right began a rather steep incline up. The shaft or tunnel going to the left seemed to be going down. The intersection was reinforced with large timbers, which supported the roof and side walls.

Reggie moved forward past the troop of single-file boy scouts. The shafts had opened up and now had plenty room for two, three, or even four people to walk side by side. The ceiling was now high enough to where even a horse or mule could travel.

Randy looked at Regg as he came up to the intersection to examine the find. The timbers looked sturdy enough. The rock looked solid. It didn't look dangerous at all.

"What do you think?" Reggie asked out loud.

The group of eight scouts now closed in so they formed a small huddle, their little headlights searching up and down the now three shafts. The tunnel they had just come out of was a smaller single-file shaft. It joined what looked like a main working shaft big enough for horses pulling carts, which came from higher on the right, going lower to the left.

There were also more markings on the walls. Some were obvious miner markings with letters scratched into the stone. They were dates with initials. One date read "1836." To the right of the date were the initials "JD" and "ES." To the side of that, there were more markings and stick painting that looked like Native American writings and drawings.

"If my memory serves me correctly, Michigan didn't officially become a state until October of 1837," Randy said, looking thoughtfully at the carved characters in the rock wall.

One of the scouts flashed a picture. His phone was able to capture the scribing with Randy and Reggie standing there looking like archeologists who had just discovered some ancient mummy.

"Just a guess," Randy said, "but I bet the tunnel going up to the right might lead to the top of the mountain. The shaft to the left going down might lead to the actual dig site or maybe a vein of whatever was being mined here."

Reggie moved about ten feet in both directions, first down to the left and then to the shaft going up to the right. Meanwhile, the scouts were taking pictures of one another standing next to the mining and Indian hieroglyphics that decorated the wall. Randy watched as Reggie tested the shaft in each direction. Definitely a brighter and more active torch flame when going up to the right. That would be the way to an exit or opening.

"Okay, guys, let's take a break here and discuss our next move. I think we might be getting close to an opening in this mine shaft," Reggie proclaimed as he set down his backpack and eyed Randy, as in saying, "Team huddle."

Most of the boys had already taken off their light packs and set them on the rock cavern floor so they could take their National Geographic photos with the rock wall scrawlings. Randy and Reggie picked a clear space on the rock floor, took a brief swig of water, and then concentrated on the spread-out map, squinting with the light of their LED headlamps. Randy moved the point of a small stick along the map, tracing what he thought might have been their underground route on the surface. Their GPSs lost what little signal they had once they penetrated the rock burrow.

"Based on our pace count and the direction I think we were heading," Randy started, "I think we should be right about here." He was pointing to a place on the map contours that placed them just inside the Huron Mountain Club boundary marks indicated on the map sheet.

"I agree," replied Reggie. "At least should be close to that point. Then from there, we have high ground and should be able to get a phone and GPS signal."

The group was already twenty-four hours late for contact, and rangers should be headed into their last contact point in the McCormick Wilderness Area near Summit Lake.

All the scouts were finished taking pictures for photos they were sure would end up on the cover of National Geographic Magazine or at least on the front pages of all the local newspapers. Everyone had the opportunity to drink some water and take a few bites of whatever snacks were still left in their day packs.

Randy and Reggie stood up to announce the plan.

"Okay, guys, here's the deal," began Randy. "We think the shaft going up leads to surface opening on high ground. From there, we should be able to get a cell phone signal and GPS signal. We are already twenty-four hours late for our last check-in call, and chances are there are forest service rangers already on their way up to Summit Lake where we last made phone contact."

Reggie chimed in now, "The plan is to make contact with Amanda and Claire at base camp to let them know we are all right, then talk with forest ranger Tony Lindeman. We will tell Lindeman about the body so he can start coordinating with law enforcement and extraction of the remains."

Randy took over the plan briefing from there. "We will also call Mrs. McCormick that we think we found her lost mine shaft."

At that, the scouts started doing rounds of high fives to celebrate "mission accomplished."

Reggie spoke up now. "Okay, gang, we move out again in five minutes. Pack up, check your equipment, and be ready to move out."

Several of the boys had to relieve themselves, so they stepped down the shaft into the shadowy murkiness. The LED headlamps cut narrow beams into the gull of darkness, which seemed to expand as it when down. The boys were talking excitedly as they walked and heard one of the scout leaders' call for them to "not go too far." The boys smirked at one another, and one said softly, "Ya, like where could we go down here?" which was followed by the group chuckling collectively.

The adolescent penis artists were drawing squiggly lines of urine art in the dusty rock floor when the first noises came. At first, there was a soft, slow shuffle on rock. Anthony, a muscular boy with dark hair, heard the subtle noise first.

"Shhh!" hushed Anthony to the rest of the group, who were still giggling and chatting it up to see who could shoot their yellow stream the farthest. They all went quiet except for Sam Hubble, who had won the "distance contest" and was still pissing.

Everyone shut up, and the only noises were the distant chatting of the rest of the group up the shaft and Sam trying to finish off taking a leak. Now there was the soft shuffling sound and a low guttural moan. At the sound of the moan, Sam turned as if to run and pissed all over Anthony and one of the other boys. He also pissed all over himself.

Anthony cursed and demanded everyone to wait as he took lead by shining his headlamp in the direction of the noises. It took a couple seconds, but the group of boys regained their courage and began shining their lights down the passage, bouncing the beams off the walls, floor, and ceiling.

Dusty bones, deer antlers, and even a few what appeared to be human skulls littered the cavern floor. There it was again, the slow shuffle and guttural groan. Light beams all focused on the direction of the noise.

The slow-moving form almost blended into the cavern wall. Then shape started taking place, strands of matted gray and brown hair, a large deer antler, and now a louder, deeper growling groan. The form seemed to be moving toward them. Yep, the boys were done pissing.

Poor Sam Hubble had caught his willy whacker in his zipper. In his haste to evacuate their current predicament, he missed tucking his boyhood all the way in before zipping up. Sam's painful scream accelerated the panic enveloping the small group of "urine artists" as now a couple boyish screams of terror chimed in with Sam's scream of pain.

Both Reggie and Randy's heads jerked toward the down shaft as they heard the screams and saw the frenzied panic of the oncoming boys.

"What the…!" started Randy but he was cut off by almost being trampled by the oncoming rush of boys. The panic hit the rest of the scouts like an oncoming whirlwind, and they were caught up scrambling toward the up shaft and probable mine entrance. Randy and Reggie looked at each other, puzzled and questioning whether to run or stand and fight. They couldn't see anything coming, and half the boys had left their packs scattered on the shaft floor.

This wasn't good. Randy knew it. "Go round up the boys and meet me in about a hundred feet or the mouth of the mine shaft," Randy told Reggie. They needed to get control of the panicking boys before someone got hurt.

Randy continued, "I'll go see what the panic is all about and I will pick up the packs on the way up. Make sure everyone is okay and that we have all the scouts accounted for."

Reggie nodded and then moved quickly up the shaft in the direction of the panicking herd of scouts. Reg and Randy worked well together as a team. Depending on circumstances, one would take the lead and the other would follow. This was Randy taking the lead now, and Reggie was relieved that he was.

It was about 250 feet up the shaft to hit daylight and the opening of the mine. Daylight and fresh air must have brought reality back to the panic-stricken troop. By the time Reggie arrived at the mine shaft opening, all the boys were together and talking wildly, still unsure of what was moving in the dark below.

"What the hell was that!" scolded Reggie.

Anthony spoke up as group panic started turning to group embarrassment. "We saw something in the cave." Anthony was now trying project a calm but firm voice.

"What did you see?" Reggie asked, this time with more compassion rather than scold in his voice.

Again Anthony answered, "We're not sure, but it had hair, antlers, and was growling!" All eyes now were looking at one another as if to justify their panic.

"Okay," said Reggie, "you all stay right fricking here until we come back! I'm going back to help Randy bring up the rest of your packs. It's possible it was a bear, so stay here. In the meantime, make the cell phone call to base camp to let them know we are okay. Also, give them this grid coordinate to pass on to the forest rangers who are on their way." He then tossed Anthony a GPS and disappeared back down the mine shaft entrance.

The mine shaft hadn't been sealed off like most of the old shafts in the Upper Peninsula. In fact, the entrance looked well maintained, like it was still being used. To add more questions to the *puzzle*, it looked like an old two-track leading away from the opening and toward another outcrop of rocks in a northwesterly direction, toward what would be the interior of the Huron Mountain Club area.

Randy had moved cautiously down the mine shaft in the direction the panicked boys had evacuated. He knew that it was possible the boys ran into a bear, a raccoon, or even a deer that somehow got trapped in the tunnel. After about thirty feet or so, Randy heard the soft shuffle and deep groans. He shined and focused his headlamp to get it centered on the location of the noise. It wasn't a bear, a raccoon, or even a deer. There in the dark was a poor soul of a man, still alive, but covered in matted dirt and with disheveled gray hair and a long grimy beard. He was wearing animal furs and propping himself up with a wooden staff topped with a deer antler as a handle.

The ancient man could hardly move and appeared to be injured. Randy moved slowly forward toward the struggling old man and asked if he was okay. Blind eyes were all that peered back and a low guttural groan. The man looked like he was starving, and one ankle was bleeding badly as if he had been chained up by that ankle.

Randy half-yelled for the old man to stay put as he ran back up the shaft to get help. Reggie was already on his way down, and they almost collided.

It took a total of ten minutes for Reggie to run back up to the shaft opening, have the scouts make a field-expedient litter, and get the entire troop back down the shaft to assist in evacuating the old-timer from the mine shaft.

Meanwhile, Randy went back and had the old man sit down while he gave him some water and applied first aid to the ankle wound. Not only did the poor old guy appear to be blind, but his tongue was missing, so he couldn't talk. The leathered crease on his face and hands told the story of weathered skin and a life of hard work and outdoor exposure.

"Just who is this guy?" Randy said out loud to no one in particular later that night as the group warmed themselves around the campfire.

They had managed to litter-carry the old fella out of the mine shaft, set up a temporary camp near the shaft opening complete with a fire and makeshift beds with shelters, find a water source nearby, and kill a porcupine for supper—all before dark.

Earlier, the scouts had called into Amanda and Claire at base camp to check in and give an update. Needless to say, worried mothers were relieved. The scouts also passed on the grid location of their position to ranger Tony Lindeman and the two other forest rangers who were already packing in to locate the group of Adventure Bound Scouts.

Randy and Reggie had called Amanda and Claire to let them know about the old-timer they found in the mine shaft and asked them to pass the word on to the forest rangers who were working their way through the McCormick Wilderness Area to their location. About thirty minutes had passed when Amanda called back, informing Randy that they couldn't make contact with forest ranger Lindeman.

The dancing flames of the group's campfire had settled down into a bed of hot embers now. It was 11:00 p.m. and still no forest rangers. The tattered old man they found down in the mine shaft was lying uncomfortably on a bed of branches, spruce bows, and leaves. He had a survival space blanket underneath him and covering him. Reggie and Randy tried to get him as comfortable as possible, but nothing was working. Randy had mentioned to Reggie that he wondered if maybe the old guy had some broken ribs or internal injuries. They just had to get the man through the night, and then with any luck, they would be able to air evacuate him out tomorrow during daylight when the weather cleared.

One of the scouts placed a couple of broken tree limbs on the hot embers and was about to toss in a board of wood with writing on it. Randy saw the board and asked the scout to hand it to him.

The wooden board seemed old, very old, maybe as ancient as the old fella lying between the space blankets. Randy looked closer at the board, turning it so the scrawling could be read by the light of the fire. Both Reggie and Randy looked at the writing, which looked like it had been etched with a sharp stone. Together they both read it out loud, "Doom!"

Chapter 22

GATHERING OF FORCES

Jake Catrin made a few phone calls before taking off in his pickup truck for Marquette to meet up with Caden. Jake had contacts in the CIA and FBI—fellow soldiers from his days in the military who went on to jobs in law enforcement and spying. Jake didn't like what he was being told about the Astor family. They were politically connected, had deep pockets, and were well connected practically everywhere. Jake remembered seeing a scandal here and there about the Astors on national television, but he didn't really pay much attention to all the political rhetoric. What got his attention most, however, was a buddy in the FBI who told him that the Astor coverups made the Clinton coverups look like a girl scout cookie sale.

Jake knew that this news of the ruthlessness of the Astor family meant there would be a good chance of people getting killed along with a media and political coverup favoring the Astors. Jake had a trump card, however, and he let the right people know what was going on with the disappearances, the coverups, and crooked cops in Marquette, Michigan. Jake sped the hour and a half to Marquette confident that when the proverbial "shit hit the fan," which he was sure would, they would have powerful people, federal law enforcement, and unbiased media in their corner.

For now, however, the clock was ticking, and his daughter's life was in jeopardy. There was no way outside help would be able to get there in time to save Kat and whoever else this Dirk Astor character and his goons had at the Huron Mountain Club.

Thank God we still have a Second Amendment in America, Jake thought to himself as he pulled in Caden's apartment building.

When Jake Catrin stepped in Caden Garrett's apartment, Caden and Mingo had a map of the Huron Mountain Club spread out on a table and were poring over all the information they could gather on the Huron Mountain Club, Dirk Astor, and the Astor family. Caden had reached the same conclusion as Jake about the Astor family, their power, money, and crooked connections. This wasn't going to be easy, and it would probably have national-level news implications.

Meanwhile, at the Marquette airport, Sawyer International Airport, the first private plane had arrived with a mob "cleanup crew" and a dozen ex-military types whom Dirk had asked for by name. These guys were good, loyal to the Astor dollar, and ruthless. Dirk had seen these guys in action before and was impressed.

Another private Astor plane would be arriving at Sawyer International Airport within twenty-four hours with another fifteen security goons who were loyal to Astor money. These were the typical Astor security personnel, who had no scruples when it came to *bending* the law. After all, the law was *subjective*, and money and power would always beat *common folk*. Additionally, the elder Astor, Jack Astor, Dirk's father, would send two reporters, also on the Astor payroll, who would "cover the news releases" and make sure any press was favorable to the Astor name, or counter any negative news. The media was "just in case" Dirk's "problem" couldn't be contained locally.

Chapter 23

PRISONERS

Kat opened her eyes, but there was nothing but darkness. Her brain was groggy and disoriented as she tried to focus and make out something in the darkness. Her hands were tied behind her back, and one ankle seemed to be shackled with a locking ankle collar attached to a chain, which seemed to be attached to the wall somehow. She had been half-slumped over, sitting down on a wooded floor. She moved her leg again and felt the tension as the links gave a metallic rattle.

On the other side of the black space she was in, she heard the stirring of another metallic chain.

"Who's there?" Kat said in a whisper. There was no response at first, only some more sound of the chain slowly moving.

"Kat, is that you!" came the reply in the dark.

It was Sydney Willington's voice, and it was weak and shaky. Kat asked if she was all right and if Troy was with her. Sydney confirmed it was her and said Troy was there but that he was hurt pretty bad. At that, there was another rattling of chains and a soft groan of pain.

Sydney and Troy were tied up and chained in the darkness, too, as Syd tried to explain to Kat what happened to them.

Sydney and Troy had been invited to a party by some guy at the Wooden Nickle, a nice enough guy, or so they thought. All they remembered was leaving the Wooden Nickle with the guy and some of his friends and then waking up here in this old cabin chained up.

"That son of a bitch!" Kat exhaled, again trying to focus and sit up straight.

Outside, through an old six-pane, dusty window, the breaking light of the sun started crawling up a craggy, mountainous horizon.

Syd and Troy had been there since last Sunday morning, at least that was when they woke up. Troy had been beat up pretty bad when he tried to escape a couple days ago. His jaw was broken, it felt like he had a couple broken ribs, and one of his shoulders was out of socket. Sydney had been smacked in the face a couple times by an older guy who would check on them a couple times a day to give them a little food and water and let them go to the rustic outhouse to relieve themselves. He was a cruel geezer who seemed to enjoy seeing his prisoners suffer.

"We need to get out of here," Kat pleaded urgently. "I think these are the same guys who killed Nadia and are responsible for Erik's disappearance!"

"They have to be," replied Sydney. "The last we saw them was last Sunday night when they were giving Mr. Personality instructions on what to do with us."

"Right," said Kat. "This is not going to end well for us if we don't get out of here. And we need to do it sooner rather than later!"

With that, the three prisoners began struggling to get free and make their escape.

The gathering light outside made it somewhat easier but still not easy. Kat wasn't going to be kept prisoner by this asshole Asher. She was gaining her senses now and she was more angry than afraid. With a twist and forced strain on her tied hands, she felt her thumb pop out of joint. She winced in pain but continued working the hand to get it free. Finally, her hands were free. Now all she needed to do was get free of this ankle bracelet.

With the gathering light, Kat was able to make out objects in the old log shed. With the assortment of tools, benches, buckets, and a long worktable, it looked like an old storage shed or maybe even an old repair shed. On the floor about five feet away and tucked up against the wall, there looked to be an old knife blade without any handle. Stretching out, her body extending from her chained leg, she was just able to reach the blade. Within a matter of thirty minutes and some careful cutting, Kat was able to work her way free from the heavy leather ankle bracelet attached to the chain.

Moving quickly to Sydney and Troy, she first cut the ropes securing their hands then gave the knife to Sydney to free herself and Troy. Kat needed to get a look outside and try to figure out where they were.

Chapter 24

MINE SHAFT #5

The plan for the morning, according to the two Adventure Bound Scout leaders, was to assist with the air evacuation of the blind old-timer to Marquette General Hospital for emergency care. They would then guide the Marquette County sheriff to the body at the bottom of the cliff. After those tasks were completed, they would head by to their main camp with all their gear and head back to base camp at Craig Lake State Park and the anxiously waiting Amanda Adams and Claire Peterson.

What's the old saying about "The best-laid plans of mice and men…" or the one the military has about a plan for combat, "The plan never survives the first contact"? Yep, plans change, and so it would be with the scouts.

It was still dark, maybe three thirty or four in the morning, when scout leader Reggie Townsend got up to throw a few pieces of wood on the fire and take a piss. It took a few minutes to realize their rescue subject, the old blind man, was missing from his space blanket bed. Reggie looked around and listened for any sounds of movement in the underbrush. Nothing. That was strange.

Reggie sat by the fire poking the hot coals to excite the flame a little. He was fully expecting the old-timer to come back in from the darkness to the sound of the crackling flames. A couple minutes went by and there was still nothing, no returning old soul who just needed to relieve himself.

Satisfied the old man was "missing," Reggie shook Randy's shoulder, who had just *finally* gone off to sleep but now woke with a start.

Sleepy, tired eyes from Randy met Reggie's excited look. "He's gone! The old guy is gone!"

Randy looked around the camp circle of sleeping bodies and saw the empty space blanket where the old man was supposed to be. "Where is he?" Randy asked, still half asleep and, by this time, totally confused.

Reggie explained that he didn't know and only discovered the old man missing after getting up to check the fire and take a leak. The two exchanged puzzled looks, and now Randy got up to help solve the mystery of the missing man.

The two scout leaders walked small circles around the campsite, using their LED headlights to peer in the dark shadows of trees, rocks, and underbrush…nothing. Randy was searching in the direction away from the mine shaft in which they had emerged, half following the trail that seemed to lead away from the shaft. In the underbrush, Randy saw something gray and lying flat on the ground.

"Reggie, there is something here!" Randy called as he walked closer, keeping his light focused on the object in question.

Pushing aside the underbrush, Randy pushed the object with the tow of his boot. The leaves rustled, exposing what appeared to be a long wooden sign. The two scout leaders looked at each other, and then Reggie reached down to pick it up.

Huron Mountain Club Property, Keep Out!

Under that sign was another wood sign, which read "HMC Property, Shaft #5."

"Do you think this is from the shaft we came out of?" Randy asked.

Reggie shrugged his shoulders and pointed to the remnants of the old trail leading away from their campsite and the shaft. They followed about thirty yards and came up to another rock outcropping. There it was, another mine shaft, and still attached to one of the entrance timbers was a sign that read "HMC Property, Keep Out!" Randy and Reggie looked at each other with disbelief.

"Whoa!" Randy exclaimed. "I think we might be trespassing on Huron Mountain Club property now. Maybe we better get back to the boys and get them involved in the search for the old guy."

Reggie nodded in agreement, and they headed back to the campfire and the scout troop. The sun would be starting to push the first rays of light up soon, so it would be a good time to rouse everyone up.

All the boys were up now, and the fire was still crackling. The sun still hadn't started making its appearance yet.

The sudden sounds cut through the dark like nails scratching a chalkboard. First, there were the bloodcurdling screams, human they all would later think. Then there was the guttural roar with gnashing of flesh, more human screaming in terror, then animal-like growling with a violent shaking of the brush like a crocodile that had just caught a wildebeest trying to cross a riverbed. The sounds originated from the direction of the mine shaft they had explored and emerged from the day before, but it didn't sound like it was in the tunnel. Eyes were all filled with terror now, even Reggie's and Randy's.

Whatever was happening was not good. The two scout leaders looked at each other in dismay with the feeling of impending doom closing in on them. The late forest rangers and the old man would have to wait. At this very moment, survival seemed more important than a search.

Randy yelled, "Let's go, follow me!"

The safest direction seemed to be away from the screams and sounds of carnage. Randy led, Reggie picking up the rear and making sure all the boys were moving and accounted for. Randy thought that the newly discovered mine shaft must lead to the Huron Mountain Club grounds and from there safety, at least that's what he hoped. Moving quickly in the darkness through the trees and underbrush could more than likely put them at the top of a cliff with nowhere to go except a long drop like the poor hunter they found yesterday.

So with headlamps on again and moving with the purpose of not encountering what was causing the hair-raising screams, the Adventure Bound Scouts once again scrambled into a mine shaft with more questions than answers.

With the last of the scout troop disappearing into the trees and darkness, the two prankster forest rangers stepped out into the opening by the campfire to call everyone back. The forest rangers were practically falling down with laughter now. Tony Lindeman, the lead forest ranger, decided to call the scout leaders by cell phone to call the prank off, but it was too late. The scouts were already in the signal dead zone of the mine shaft and moving with a purpose.

Unfortunately for the unsuspecting forest rangers, they never noticed the great antlered beast emerge from the mine shaft behind them. They were still watching in the direction the scout troop had disappeared. This time, however, the horrific screams of terror and animal carnage were not a practical joke. Blood, guts, and body parts quickly splattered on the ground near where the scouts' campfire still burned. The frenzied attack lasted only a minute. With the bloodlust completed by the great beast, it finally stared into the fire, reflecting satanic yellow eyes of pure evil. Its matted fur was covered in blood and gore, along its werewolf-looking face, muscled arms and legs, and razor-sharp talons. Standing on its two hind legs, it then looked at the horizon and the last of the dying moon. As it did, it arched its head back to bellow a howling scream that silenced everything in the dying night. Now, with the first signs of morning nautical twilight, it quickly disappeared into the mine shaft from where it came. Behind it, this beast of Indian lore, were two lifeless bodies, or what was left of them, dragged to be ravished by an insatiable hunger within the darkness and safety of the cave.

Chapter 25

RESCUE PLAN

Caden, Jake, and Mingo had spent three hours studying the layout of the Huron Mountain Club on an old site map and the terrain in and around the club boarders on a topographic map. They didn't have any aircraft support for an insertion and extraction, so this was going to have to be an operation conducted on foot, vehicles, all-terrain vehicles (ATVs), or most likely a combination of all three.

Caden and Jake had taken a pair of Jake's four-wheelers, ATVs, onto trails that led around Eagle Mine grounds, which sat, ironically, south of the Huron Mountains and east of the McCormick Wilderness Area. They found the opening with a high point, which they had identified on their topo maps back at the apartment. The site was suitable to launch their drone to conduct an aerial reconnaissance of the HMC grounds and perimeter; they had guessed correctly that the club grounds would be protected by a metal chain length fence, security cameras, and roving security patrols.

Mingo and Nina drove Troy's old van up County Road KK to get within walking distance and then viewing distance of the main guarded entrance to the Huron Mountain Club. Luckily, Troy had given Caden a spare set of keys, which Caden forgot to return. Based on information gathered from all the maps, this would be the only vehicle entrance to the grounds. The only other entry point would be by boat from Lake Superior. Mingo and Nina would surveil the main road entrance for activity, while Caden and Jake would check out the Lake Superior docking area with the drone.

The two recon parties each carried both cell phones and satellite phones, which Jake had brought in his *little* bag of tricks. Actually, Jake's "little bag of tricks" was several boxes and gear bags that included a couple of drones, night optics, and an assortment of small arms with matching ammo—enough for an *ugly* rescue mission. The gear supply list also included an assortment of explosives. Jake wasn't taking any chances. If these kidnappers wanted to get rough, then they had just walked into Jake, Caden, and Mingo's "playground."

Meanwhile, back at Caden and Mingo's apartment, Mrs. Catrin, Susan Catrin, had arrived. She started organizing to be the mission Tactical Operations Center, or TOC as Jake called it. She, along with Nina, would keep track of the progress of the rescue mission and also brief the FBI when they arrived.

Jake's friend and contact in the FBI, John Anderson, had gone out on a limb for Jake by putting together a team to come in and take over the investigation from the local law enforcement. They would come in *unannounced* as to not give away their intent in advance. Even now, however, two requests for search warrants of the Huron Mountain Club had been denied. It was now becoming painfully obvious to FBI Agent John Anderson just how well connected, both politically and within the law enforcement community, the Astors and the Huron Mountain Club were, in fact. Anderson decided to not inform their local Marquette FBI contacts of their arrival either, at least until they were there in person. At this point, it was unclear on just how deep the local law enforcement corruption went. It was better to come in quick and unexpected as to not tip off any corrupt officials. It would still be another twenty-four hours before they could arrive. The FBI bureaucracy seemed to moving against their every effort.

It was now 3:00 p.m., or 1500 hours, the designated linkup time back at Caden Garrett's apartment. Caden and Jake entered the apartment door to see Susan Catrin just finishing setting up their TOC. Caden looked at Jake, his eyebrows raised as if half surprised.

Jake winked back at Caden, simply saying, "Yep, she's done this before," then chuckling to himself.

Susan walked up to each and gave a warm hug, her eyes furrowing with concern. Five minutes later, Mingo and Nina would enter the apartment, to be met with the same warm embrace and looks of concern.

Susan sat them all down at the kitchen counter to a late lunch of pasties with gravy, a popular Yooper meal, which looked like a pie sandwich and contained a variety of vegetables, potatoes, and any choice of an assortment of meats, depending on one's tastes.

They needed to share information from their recons, refine their options, and come up with a workable plan. They didn't have much time. Everyone was in agreement that they needed to get in as soon as possible to get Kat. The more time that went by, the less her chances of survival. Jake, Caden, and Mingo had been on enough rescue missions to know this simple fact.

In turn, they talked while the others ate and listened.

Mingo and Nina briefed the "in and out" traffic patterns, guard shifts, number of guards, how well they were armed, barriers, a hidden location to get through the fence a couple hundred meters from the guard shack and other details. They had also observed two vans, one an HMC van and the other a Marquette airport van, which were filled with about fifteen to twenty military-aged men. The airport van departed the grounds about fifteen minutes later—empty. The HMC van looked as if it remained on the grounds.

Caden and Jake had found an obscured fence location where they could cut the fence undetected by any security cameras or roving guards. Most of their observation information, however, came from the drone. The interior of HMC, from the entry gate to the cabin complex, had a nice paved road. Off the main vein road, there were treks of well-groomed gravel or paved roads that went to various property lakes, picnic sites, or trailheads. Most of the camp was wooded and varied in terrain, so once in, foot movement without detection wouldn't be a problem.

The Lake Superior dock area had some walking traffic from the ritzy but rustic main housing area. Likewise, a few people walked some of the trails and roads from the housing area to trailheads, probably hiking to some of the fantastic lakes and views on the property. Luckily, the busy time of July and August visitors was over, so the people count was way down, except beefed-up security that had arrived from the Marquette airport. They needed to avoid any collateral damage, both of people and of buildings.

They had also identified a maintenance area, which contained vehicle stables with four Mercedes Rovers, a couple black sedans, four vans, two pickup trucks, and several ATVs. There was also a maintenance garage and a couple other smaller outbuildings.

Every place on the main housing complex area seemed to have too many people to be holding any captives, unless, of course, everyone there was in on the kidnapping, which Jake and Caden doubted.

Of particular interest, they noticed one ATV take an obscure trail to a far-corner boundary of the HMC and stop at a remote, solitary cabin. The drone was able to follow the solitary rider without being detected up to the cabin, which was about a twenty-minute trip. The building didn't fit same attention to detail of well-kept and maintained status, which seems to be the standard for all facilities of these elite mega-rich owners of the HMC. It also seemed unusual that this building was located almost on the boarder of HMC grounds and would have an ATV trail leading to it. The whole purpose of the Huron Mountain Club was to be an exemplary conservancy of UP wilderness with minimal and restricted vehicle traffic.

The group finally finished up the meal and briefings from the reconnaissance trips earlier that day. The group then moved to the map sheet of HMC laid out on the table and the large topo map taped to the wall. The group moved back and forth from the wall to the table as they pointed out exactly where locations were on the maps that they had discussed during their recon back briefs. The discussions went back and forth and around the group. Finally, they decided on a course of action that they thought would provide their greatest chances of success while minimizing collateral damage. They didn't have nearly enough people, so they would have to improvise. They would need two or three diversions, and they would need to be able to travel quickly once inside the HMC property. Exfiltration from the club grounds would either have to be quick and unexpected, through the main gate or stealthy on foot. Both contingencies would have to be planned.

Additionally, the aftermath of getting Kat out of the kidnapper's custody would have to be thought out, especially now that they knew there were corrupt cops within the Marquette municipality and that the rich elites of the club would do damage control and try to make them look like the criminals. Jake was putting a lot of trust in his FBI friend, John Anderson, to do most of the damage control on their behalf.

Chapter 26

SURPRISE MEETING

Kat peered out of a dusty window from the old log toolshed. Syd worked vigorously on the thick leather ankle bracelet, which had her chained to the wall. Troy sat slumped over against a wall, hands untied but ankle bracelet with chain still intact.

No one seemed to be outside the old cabin. She had tried the door, but it was chain-locked from the outside. To the front of the cabin, an old two-track led downhill and away. In the back of the old cabin, boulders and trees rose up out of site. The old dusty windows were *slide-ups*, and maybe she could fit through one, Kat thought to herself as she worked the old six-pane window to the up position. She grabbed one of the old benches, using it as a step stool, and hoisted herself up and through the window. Tumbling to the ground, she then jumped up to take a quick look around, only to see a side-by-side ATV coming up the old two-track.

Kat didn't have time to think. She saw the man was armed with both a sidearm and a long rifle. Ducking out of view behind the cabin, she then made a beeline for the rising trees and boulders behind the cabin. Within a minute, the guy was back out the door and looking frantically in all directions. Kat heard the man curse loudly. She heard the man talking frantically to himself about Dirk Astor killing him if he didn't get the prisoner back. The old man now slowed his gaze, trying to regain his composure and peering behind the cabin up into the trees and boulders.

The shot happened quickly. Kat didn't know the guy could see her, but he obviously did. The bullet hit a rock a foot from Kat's head and spit fragments of rock chips at her, pelting her dirt-covered shirt. She turned quickly, keeping a large boulder between her and the shooter as she scrambled up what looked like an old goat path. Forty yards up a steep zig-zag incline and she came to an opening in the rock face.

She looked left and then right. Nowhere to go that that would conceal her from the shooter. The rock face was too steep to climb, so it would have to be into the cave. She looked back to see the man look at the open window, look up in her direction, and then start clambering uphill toward her position.

"Crap," Callie Catrin muttered to herself. *No flashlight, no matches, no torch. Into the dark it would have to be*, Kat thought to herself.

With that, she began working her way along the cave wall, eventually feeling her way into the welcoming darkness. Better the darkness than getting shot at, Kat kept telling herself as she crept deeper into the well of darkness.

As Kat worked her way into the cave system, which started a steep incline up, the Adventure Bound Scout troop was working its way down the same main shaft.

Randy was still leading the troop with Reggie picking up the rear of the group. Their hurried pace had slowed now to a cautious walk. They had stopped several times, turned off all their lights, and listened for any sounds that might be following them. Nothing. Hopefully the terror that they heard earlier wasn't coming after them.

The group had gone about one thousand yards down mine shaft #5 and was still descending in a downward direction. Randy heard the quiet shuffling up ahead and froze. The next trailing scout bumped into Randy, almost knocking him over.

"Shhh!" Randy cautioned the trail of scouts, holding his hand up in the air to get everyone to stop and be quiet.

Everyone went dead silent, but all LED headlamps were pointing forward down the dark tunnel. The memory of running into the old-timer in the other mine shaft was still fresh in everyone's minds. Everyone was on full alert, not knowing what to expect. Fight-or-flight instincts were ready to rock and roll and kick into full gear.

Kat slowly shuffled forward into the dark, moving slowly in the pitch dark. Suddenly, very faintly, she heard scuffling on the rock floor as if a giant caterpillar were steadily working its way down the tunnel ahead in her direction. Kat froze solid. A guy was trying to shoot her coming from behind, and this terrorizing sound was moving toward her from ahead with nowhere to go.

Kat squinted into the darkness. Was that light that she could see reflecting off the shaft walls? She edged forward to verify if it was, in fact, light. The sound had now stopped, and there seemed to be a brief moment of whispers. The light, or now lights, were bouncing of the cave walls as if searching for something.

Reggie had moved to the front of the troop and was now standing beside Randy.

"What do you think, Randy?" asked Reggie.

Randy stared blankly back at his fellow scout leader. Finally, Randy called out, "Is anybody there? We are a scout troop!"

Kat heard the male voice call out. *Scout troop?* she thought to herself. "Hello!" she called back.

Reggie and Randy moved forward toward the female voice. She had the tone of distress and caution in her voice. Reggie called out now, "We are a scout troop from Crystal Falls, we can help you!"

Kate squinted in disbelief as the group slowly moved toward her, lights bouncing all over and shining in her eyes, blinding her to what was closing in on the spot she was standing.

"Are you okay?" Randy asked. "Okay, guys, stop shining your lights in her face," he ordered back to the group.

Callie Catrin studied the group with caution but with growing optimism. "You are a scout troop from Crystal Falls?" she asked in disbelief. "Did you get lost?" she asked, realizing the strange irony of her question as soon as she blurted it out.

Randy asked again if she was okay, ignoring her feeble attempt at humor.

The Adventure Bound Scout troop listened with intense focus as Kat tried to explain her dilemma and how she ended up in this specific spot right now—the drugging, the kidnapping, being tied up and chained to the wall, the old ruffian shooting at her, and with Syd and Troy still being prisoners back in the old shed.

The newly formed group discussed options briefly and decided the best course of action was to head back down the shaft toward the single gunman and the still captured Troy and Sydney. There wasn't a good choice to be made here, only a decision with the best chance of getting help. The scouts' *adventure* had now turned more into a survival situation. Confronting the gunman would be dangerous, but it was also possible he didn't follow into the cave.

At the opening of the cave, Reggie and Randy looked out and saw no one. They moved farther out, far enough to see the old cabin down below. No gunman and no ATV parked by the single building. The remainder of the group moved out into the trees and boulders to get a better view. Randy slowly crept down to the storage building, staying alert for the first sign of danger. Everything seemed to be clear of danger for now. From alongside the building, Randy waved for the rest of the group to come down.

The group assembled in the old storage cabin. Sydney and Troy were gone, but the chains and cut leather ankle bracelets lay, now docile, on the floor. Randy and Reggie looked at each other, grave looks of concern filling their faces. Kat moved around the room, now searching for any signs of what happened and anything they could use for what was to come.

Kate now eyed a closet door in the corner that she had missed earlier. She walked up and opened the creaky door and almost jumped back with what she first thought was a live animal inside. Randy and the rest of the group noticed her reaction and moved near to get a better look.

Hanging on a coat hook was what looked like a werewolf mask with an antlered, fur-covered head covering. There was also a straggly-looking fur suit or covering with two long claw-tipped fake arms attached.

"What the…!" Reggie exclaimed as he reached and pulled the costume from the closet. The mask was scary and realistic with two yellow eyes and slits large enough for the wearer to see out. The fake claw-ended arms would be held by extended handles from underneath the fur covering. The claws were real enough and capable of shredding flesh if yielded as a weapon from underneath the fur coverings. The antlers, on the other hand, were of a firm rubbery material, which could be folded or collapsed in the locker but recoil to a massive set of antlers when worn upon the head as a helmet-like head covering with a chin strap.

Kat exclaimed "Now this would scare the crap out of you!"

The boys in the troop responded with nervous chuckles and glances at one another. Yes, running into this *creature* in the dark would be enough to scare someone stiff. If that didn't do it, then the slashing arms could cause real enough harm.

Finding the terrorizing costume in the closet threw everyone in the group into a moment of puzzled paralysis. The mystery of this place, the kidnapping, the costume, the man shooting at Kat now swirled in the group's collective mind. There were more questions than answers. One thing was for sure, however—the danger they were in was very real.

The scouts scrounged the building for anything that could be used for survival. Reggie and Randy went outside, attempting to reach the forest rangers and their base camp by cell phone. No service. The GPS hit on three satellites and gave them a pretty accurate indication of their location.

No communications and a crazy man with a gun did not leave many good options. The hike down to the main housing area of the Huron Mountain Club would take four to five hours at best, from what they could determine. Would they run into more *unfriendly* gun-yielding people or would they be met by people willing to help? If they went back up through the mine shaft to the top of this mountain, they would have communications, but would they run into the unknown *terror* at the top again? That was, of course, if there really was something up there or a prank or someone in a costume.

For now, the group decided to move to a nearby high point in a rocky outcropping, stay concealed, and continue to try making a cell phone contact. They would stay there for the time being until it got dark or the weather turned bad, and it looked like it would.

Chapter 27

TIME FOR ACTION

Outside the front gate of the Huron Mountain Club, vans were pulling up and unloading protesters with signs, megaphones, and the usual Antifa-type troublemakers wearing personal riot gear and shields. In a liberal college town like Marquette, rousing up a bunch of protester students was easy.

Susan and Nina made several anonymous calls talking about hazardous waste materials moving in and out of the Huron Mountain Club and how they were covering up a toxic waste spill. The rumor was that the toxic wastes were flowing into streams and some of the Marquette surrounding areas. The news had spread like wildfire. Even the local liberal media outlets were running with the stories without even verification. A couple of copied pictures of a hazardous waste site in another state were all the *evidence* they needed. The usual local rabble-rousers took over organization of the *flash protest,* and they planned on going well into the night. Meanwhile, the Michigan Department of Natural Recourses and their branch of the Environmental Protection Agency were fighting the local bureaucracy and political system to get emergency search warrants.

Mingo parked Troy's van at the agreed-upon location off County Road KK, about a mile from the Huron Mountain Club entry gate. He would work his way in on foot, cut through the perimeter fence, and set three remote-detonated charges. One charge was on a fuel tank, another on an old building, and another concealed on a tree near the road leading into the main lodging area. He would then sneak into a hide position overlooking a main intersection and the vehicle stalls. He would provide updates on any traffic and provide covering fire, if needed, on the intersection or vehicle stalls.

Caden and Jake had parked the black Tacoma truck near the high point they had conducted their recon from earlier. They worked their way on foot to the obscure location in the fence, cut through, and then worked their way to the HMC vehicle stalls. There was no one in the area or nearby—a good stroke of luck. Jake went to work planting remote-detonated charges, while Caden searched for keys to one of the ATVs.

Another stroke of luck—the keys were still in one of the ATVs. Caden quickly checked the fuel level, started it, and was off, tearing up the trail toward Mountain Lake. He had already preset his course on his GPS so that he could find the trek up to the cabin on the far boarder of HMC. The trek would be the same one used by the rider they had tracked earlier with the drone.

Jake set one charge in the ditch near the main intersection that led to the front gate to the living-quarters area, the vehicle stalls, and the main trail going up toward Mountain Lake. Next, he set one on the fuel pumping station. The final one he wanted to set on an old abandoned building. He walked over to check inside, but there was a chain on the door. He then shined a flashlight inside one of the windows to look around and make sure the building was, in fact, empty. As his light beam searched the darkness inside the single-room building, Jake heard a thud, which seemed to come from inside.

Jake directed his beam in the direction of the *thud* noise inside the building. There semi-hidden behind an old table which lay on its side was a shoeless foot sheathed in a grimy sock. The foot moved as the beam of light connected with it.

Someone is in there! Jake thought to himself. *Locked in there. It must be Kat!*

Jake pulled the bolt cutters out of his equipment bag and quickly cut the lock, which secured the chain holding the door closed. Quietly gliding to the old table and sock-covered foot, Jake found Sydney, hog-tied, gagged, and lying on her side. Tears had washed streaks on her dirt-covered face. Lying motionless about ten feet from Syd was Troy. He, too, was dirt-covered and shoeless. Troy looked pretty beat up, but he was still breathing.

Jake was working quickly freeing both Sydney and Troy from their bondage. Sydney was sore and bruised but she could walk. Troy, on the other hand, would need to be helped to move.

"Where is Kat?" Jake asked Syd as soon as she was ungagged.

Sydney was still disoriented from the dark, the flashlight beam, and the kick to the stomach that she had received after getting moved to this new location. She was having a hard time uttering anything coherent. Jake figured that she might have been drugged in addition to being hog-tied.

Jake finished freeing both Syd and Troy and gave them both a sip of water. Both still seemed disoriented.

Again, Jake asked Syd where Callie Catrin, Kat, was. This time, Sydney tried to focus.

"I'm not sure. In an old cabin up in the mountains" was the best Syd could produce. Burlap bags had been stuck over their heads and tied off every time they were moved.

Jake texted Susan and Nina on his cell phone. Luckily, there was still coverage near the stables. Susan and Nina were excited to hear that Jake had Syd and Troy; however, they were now concerned more than ever that he didn't have Kat. Mingo responded on the group text, "Ackn," meaning he acknowledged the message. No response from Caden.

Jake let the group know that Caden was on his way to the suspected holding building but probably wasn't there yet. Susan and Nina would keep their hopes up, uncertain if Kat would even be at the cabin on the boarder. Again, Mingo acknowledged the message. Still nothing from Caden.

Jake needed to make a decision—get Troy and Syd to safety now or stay and wait for Caden to bring Kat. Jake hadn't expected to find Syd and Troy at the vehicle stables. Still, Troy was in serious condition and looked like he needed immediate medical attention. Still nothing from Caden. Jake thought to himself that he was still probably on the move and unable to communicate.

They hadn't been compromised yet, so Jake wasn't inclined to steal a vehicle, bust through the front gate, and run over protesters to get Troy to a hospital. Although it would serve as a good diversion if Caden had Kat already, and they needed the diversion...but they didn't—not yet, anyway. Their primary plan was to accomplish this mission without being detected. Only if compromised would they go to plan B and release the army ranger's hounds of hell.

Jake tried reaching Caden by cell phone again. Still nothing. The sat phones were backup communications, but it wasn't time yet to use them. The plan was still going according to schedule. Jake texted again, this time telling the group that he was moving Syd and Troy to the primary extraction point and that he needed Susan to meet him there to pick up Syd and Troy and take them to the hospital. Texts popped back on Jake's cell phone screen. Susan acknowledged and said she was on the way. Mingo sent his "Ackn." Again, no response from Caden.

Jake had decided the best action right now was to get Troy to medical attention ASAP. Mingo could cover the intersection if needed from his position. Nina would still be at the apartment in case the team from the FBI showed up. With that, Jake hoisted Troy up, one arm over his shoulder for support, and began the slow-hobbled assist toward the fence. From the cut in the chain-link boundary fence, they would work their way up to the extraction point by the black Tacoma. Syd would remain there with Troy until Susan showed up with Jake's truck and take them to the hospital. Jake would return to the vehicle stalls and wait for Caden and Kat.

Caden had pulled the ATV off the trail about three hundred meters short of the opening, just out of sound range. Before starting up the trail toward the cabin, Caden had texted to the group that he made it to the cabin. Nothing. He was in a cell phone dead zone. If an hour passed and he was still at the cabin, he would turn on the satellite phone as agreed upon in the plan. Caden adjusted the NODs, turned them on, slung his backpack on his back, and positioned the sling carrying the M-4 rifle with the red-dot laser scope and screw-on silencer. For a little extra backup, the M-4 had an M203 grenade launcher loaded with a fléchette round mounted below the rifle's

5.56-millimeter chambered barrel. Caden wore a light-armored vest, an ammo belt with two M203 high-explosive rounds, two hand grenades, and two extra thirty-round magazines. In his light backpack were two remote detonation charges, a first aid kit, a bottle of water, and the sat phone.

"Everything a guy needed for a picnic." Caden smirked to himself as he finished loading up and starting up the trail.

The old log storage shed sat idly in the small field, backed by a rising wall of rock, trees, and a dark cloudy skyline. The wind had picked up at the higher elevation, and there was a light whipping rain. The night-vision goggles were doing their job as Caden quietly crept up the trail leading to the cabin.

Caden had seen the three ATVs parked just inside in the tree line at the opening. He placed one of his remote detonated charges out of sight but on the fuel tank of the middle ATV. He then moved to the edge of the field.

Standing behind a tree, he saw three men with scoped long rifles and flashlights come out of the front door of the cabin. Their beams of light flashed and danced here and there. First there were darting circles around on the ground, then up into the trees and rocks behind the cabin. Finally, they started following their lights toward the trees and rocky outcrop across the field from the cabin.

Caden looked up into the outcropping of rocks and trees with his night-vision goggles. Nothing. He pulled the NODs off and looked with his scope, switching it to night vision. At first, he didn't see anything. He scanned more slowly now, picking apart each rock, bump, and tree.

There it was—a slight movement in the rocks.

The three-armed men were still slowly moving across the field in the direction of the rocky outcrop when they suddenly stopped. One was talking excitedly and pointing up at the rocks. That man was also wearing night-vision optics. One of the other guys with a scoped long gun pointed up into the rocks and shot.

Now there was a scrambling sound coming from the rocky outcrop. Caden looked through his scope. It looked like about a dozen figures now dodging in a panicked manner up farther into the outcropping.

Another shot. This time, the shot was followed by a painful yell. It sounded like a kid. The group of human prey now scrambled with greater purpose. The three men were still in their halted position, but now they were all aiming up into the rocks and laughing loudly.

It only took a second for Caden to realize that these men had deadly intent. He picked out the man just getting ready to shoot. Crosshairs on the head, squeeze, *bam*. The guy slumped to the ground like a sack of dropped potatoes. Caden didn't waste any time. He shot the fléchette round at the other two, knowing it would not kill them, only pelt and disorient them. He dashed to another location about fifteen meters from his first position. Caden didn't know if there were other gunmen, but he knew it was possible. He didn't see anyone else.

Taking advantage of the disoriented gunmen, Caden positioned himself for the next shot. They were both on the ground now, talking back and forth excitedly. They were on the ground but in an open field. They would be easy targets. Caden leveled the crosshairs again, easing them to center head, squeeze, and *bang*. There was another dead lump on the ground. One more.

The last gunman, a hired hitman from New York City, couldn't hug the ground close enough. He was still searching wildly with his own rifled scope for the silenced shots that came from nowhere. The gunman heard the crashing of a branch in the tree line, quickly pointed, and shot. That was his last conscious thought as his vision went suddenly brilliant white and his head exploded into a mist of blood, skull fragments, and brain goo.

Caden had tossed a large stick over in the direction of his first shooting position. When the last gunman raised his head to get a better look and shoot, Caden squeezed off another round.

Three for three, Caden thought to himself.

Caden had moved his position again after his last shot, concealed by the trees, overcast night sky, and still drizzling rain. Caden waited. Now with his night-vision goggles back on, he scanned the old building, the tree line, and the rock outcropping for any movement. Nothing. The only sound now was the gentle wisp and occasional raindrops from the damp misting.

Caden's shots from earlier would probably go unnoticed because of his silencer. The shots from the hitmen, however, could have been heard echoing down to the Huron Mountain Club main area. Their rifles did not have any silencing devices on them. All the more reason for Caden to move quickly now and figure out the situation with this group who was the target of the three hitmen's *affections*. Caden hoped that Kat would be with them.

Convinced that there were no more shooters and not wanting to waste any time, Caden stepped out into the field and walked quickly to where the three piles of dead New York thugs lay. *Confirmed*, Caden thought to himself. Headshots were always messy.

Caden looked up to the rocky outcropping now and, walking slowly toward it, called out for Kat. He listened for a reply. Nothing. Again, moving slowly forward, he called out that he was here to help and asked if Callie Catrin was there.

Listening closely now, he could hear the excited whispers from up above in the rocks. Finally, a response came.

"Caden, is that you?" Kat's voice came from the rocky darkness.

"Kat!" Caden yelled.

Now the group of Adventure Bound Scouts and Kat started working their way down the rocky slope and toward Caden. There was excited chatter now, and Kat ran for Caden, never so happy to see anyone in all her life.

"Oh, Caden, you are a sight for sore eyes." She was almost crying as she approached her older cousin.

No one saw the end of the rifle barrel slide slowly out the window of the old log storage shed. A fourth gunman had stayed behind from the group of three with the purpose of providing any covering fire the group of three might need. He had ridden *double saddle* up the trail on one of the ATVs to the old cabin from the main lodge where the first group of New York thugs were bunking up.

Caden felt the body slam and saw stars as the round hit his body armor. He was knocked off his feet and lay on the ground with the wind knocked out of him.

"Run!" Caden croaked out as he lay on the ground, still struggling for wind.

Kat and the troop from Crystal Mountain just stood there dumbfounded.

"Run!" Caden yelled again, this time with more force.

But it was too late. A second shot rang out. Now Reggie Townsend lay bleeding, squirming on the ground, grunting out and gurgling in pain.

This time, there was no hesitation, no dumbfounded looks. Kat, along with the remainder of the Adventure Bound troop, dashed and dodged into the protective cover of the boulders going back up the rock outcropping. Another shot rang out from the building, but the only thing the bullet found was a stubborn and bulletproof boulder.

The man from the cabin came charging out now, racing past Caden, who now lay dead still. The gunman raced past Reggie Townsend, who was still wriggling on the ground in pain. The thug killer looked through his scoped rifle up into the rocks but couldn't see any movement. He then walked back to Reggie Townsend, racked another round into the chamber of his bolt action .308 caliber rifle, and turned to the outcrop of rocks.

"Come on out right now, and I won't shoot your friend here!" he yelled out.

There was no response from the rock outcropping.

"You have to in the count of ten, then I kill him!" The gunman didn't see any weapons with the group that ran into the rocks, so he was willing to bide his time for now.

He then reached into a cargo pocket of his military-style pants and produced a satellite phone. He made the call to Dirk Astor, who was waiting back at the main guest lodge.

Chapter 28

DIE TONIGHT

At the main guest lodge of the Huron Mountain Club, the young Dirk Astor, or Mr. Hottie as Kat had thought of him previously, was with his New York silver-spoon friends. All in company included the silver-spoon boys, about twenty thugs flown in from New York and some of their usual entertainment from Big Bon's, the only *gentlemen's club* or stripper club in the Upper Peninsula.

Most of the girls from Big Bon's were on Astor payroll. Half of them were, in fact, hiding from crimes they had committed in other states. It was the perfect mix of unscrupulous characters. Dirk Astor was in his element.

Dirk handed the satellite phone back to one of his bodyguard goons. Dirk had, in fact, been waiting on the call. After that idiot from the maintenance crew had let Callie Catrin escape, Dirk had sent some of his *professional boys* up to move the other two captives and hunt down this chick nicknamed Kat.

Little Kat is going to be short one more life when this night is through, Dirk thought to himself as he contemplated their next move.

"In fact," Dirk Astor said quietly to himself, "Little Kitty Kat and all her little friends are going to die tonight!"

From this latest report, three of his *pros* were dead. Three of the four he had sent up to mine shaft #5. Now, the one thug reported that two trespassers had been shot and there were at least ten more people up there, including Kat. Earlier a security camera had picked up a single rider on an ATV heading up the trail to the old mine shaft, just after dark. Then there was this bull shit protest at the main guard shack of Huron Mountain Club, protest something about toxic waste on HMC. Something was up, he knew it. He needed to find out what and he needed to be smart about it.

As far as the protest went, he already had three of his people and his media reporter infiltrate the protesters to figure out what that was about and try to get them to go away. If that didn't work, he would have some of his muscle go out, crack some heads, and have that idiot cop Ryker arrest the "rioters" for inciting violence and trespassing.

Thinking about the situation at mine shaft #5, Dirk Astor knew he needed to get more people up to the old log storage shed to "solve that problem." Dirk also suspected that if these friends of Kat, or whoever they were, had infiltrated the club grounds way up beyond Mountain Lake, they could very likely be down here in the main facility area of the club. And if they were here, chances are it would be those two rednecks from the Wooden Nickle who ruined taking their prizes Saturday night. There was still a score to settle there too. A cruel smile formed on Dirk Astor's mouth as he thought of the possibilities.

Chapter 29

TROUBLE

Mingo watched as the van carrying ten of the HMC goons came from the main housing area and went over to the vehicle stables. These guys were loaded for bear. With his night-vision scope, Mingo could see that they were all carrying military-grade, assault-style weapons with scopes, light packs, communication headsets, and flak jackets. Just an estimate, but Mingo thought there were still probably another ten or twelve of these guys still back in the lodging area.

Mingo texted on his phone to give a sitrep (situation report) on the group text. Nina texted "ackn" from their operations center (TOC) set at their apartment. Nothing from Susan, Jake, or Caden. Mingo figured that Jake and Susan were both still on their way to the linkup point at the black Tacoma. Caden was probably in a cell phone dead zone. Another fifteen minutes, they would get to sat phones if they still hadn't received word from Caden on the cell phone.

Down where all the vehicles were parked, the small band of "ready for combat" HMC soldiers were pulling out in all the remaining ATVs and side-by-side vehicles. They headed up the trail toward Mountain Lake and the far corner of the HMC property where Caden was searching for Kat.

Mingo texted in the sitrep. "Ackn," came the reply from Nina. No one else acknowledged.

"Going to sat phone in ten," came the text from Nina.

"Ackn," texted Mingo. No one else responded. Still going according to plan but this was going to be big trouble for Caden.

Chapter 30

WOUNDED SCOUTS

Caden listened as the gunman, now pointing the barrel of his rifle at Reggie Townsend's head, began his countdown from ten again. The guy had started the count twice already. Both times, a male voice from the boulders told him that they were coming out. Both times, Caden could hear Kat protest and argue. Kat knew the gunman was just going to shoot them all. Caden knew it too. The delay was a smart tactic on Kat's part, but the gunman was running out of patience.

The gunman hadn't paid any attention to Caden as he walked by. The "playing dead" rouse had worked for now. Caden knew, however, that with the sat phone call the guy had made five minutes ago, there would be reinforcement coming soon, probably in ten to fifteen minutes. Caden needed to act.

Caden's rifle was out of reach. The guy would see him before he could get to it. Caden still had a 9mm sidearm, and the guy was about fifteen paces from him. The sidearm would work. While the gunman was counting, Caden watched for the right moment to move.

"Ten, nine, eight, seven, six, five, four, three, two…!" The man counted down from ten.

"Wait!" Kat yelled as she walked out from behind the nearest boulder, walking quickly toward the gunman. The man was distracted. He knew that this young woman was the primary *kill.* He smiled cruelly as he swung the rifle barrel toward Kat with an intent to kill. He knew the Astor kid would probably give him a bonus for this one. It would be his last thought.

Caden moved quickly, rolling up to a standing position while drawing the pistol, pointing, and popping off the shots. The gunman was dead before he hit the ground—two shots to the body and one to the head.

Kat looked in disbelief at what she had just witnessed up close and personal. Some blood and brain matter had splattered on her. She was used to blood, but this, seeing a human shot up this close, was different. At that very second, she wasn't sure she would ever be able to see Caden the same way again. She knew he was the same, but now, somehow, she had changed.

Caden knew they didn't have time to waste. The wounded guy, Reggie Townsend, sounded like he had a sucking chest wound. Caden quickly stabilized the guy as best he could, keeping the punctured lung wound down, covering both the entry and exit wounds. The kid that had been shot was already patched up by the group of scouts. It was a flesh wound to a thigh muscle, and the boys had done a nice job of cleaning it up and putting a sterile covering on it. Caden looked at the wound and told the boys, "Good job."

He then instructed the group to get to the building and that there were more gunmen coming. They only have about five minutes before they arrive. Randy was quick to get the boys moving as a team, litter-carrying Reggie and getting everyone moved into the building. Kat and two of the scouts picked up the three rifles, ammunition, a sidearm, and flashlights from the dead gunmen. Caden checked the pockets of the dead men, took the sat phone, and found two sets of command-and-control headsets on the bodies, which he also took.

Once in the old cabin, Kat and Randy told Caden about the mine shaft up the mountain behind the cabin. They also told him about the strange costume in the closet, which left a puzzled look on Caden's face. Randy also explained as best and as quickly as he could how the troop ended up here, about going through the maze of mine shafts, coming in from the McCormick Wilderness Area, the missing forest rangers, and even the body at the bottom of the cliff. With the news of a body at the bottom of a cliff, Kat and Caden looked at each other and then told Randy Adams that they were missing another friend since two weeks ago.

Caden told them to try to keep Reggie as comfortable as possible and keep the punctured lung down. Caden also told them to figure out a way to get out through the back so they could get up to the mine shaft. He also told them to be prepared to get Reggie up to the mine shaft and be ready to use the weapons they had collected.

"Make no mistake," Caden tried to instill in them the gravity of the situation, "these people are intent on killing us, so we are going to have to defend ourselves."

With that, Caden grabbed his pack and his M-4 and headed out the front door. "I'll be back."

At the edge of the clearing, Caden moved to the three parked ATVs. The one that had the explosives rigged to he moved to the middle of the trail to block any high-speed assault on the cabin. Twenty meters to each side of the trail, he placed his two hand grenades, each with a trip wire attached to the pull pins. Back up the trail, another thirty meters, he set up another remote-detonated charge.

After that, he moved farther down the trail, away from the cabin. He planned on finishing this fight in the woods before it even got to the cabin. He would allow whoever was coming to get to the explosive-laced ATV, detonate it, and attack them from the rear.

Caden had just settled into his hiding position when he heard the caravan of ATVs coming up the trail. Caden watched as the group of ATVs stopped about a hundred meters short of the opening. It was difficult to see through the trees, but it looked like everyone got off their vehicle and assembled around the front ATV. After about five minutes, the caravan started up again and began moving forward. It stopped again. This time, four men split from the main group and headed out on foot—two moving along the left flank of the trail and two moving along the right flank of the trail. Additionally, two men moved slowly forward on foot up the trail toward the parked ATV with explosives. It didn't look like any of the men had night vision to Caden, but he couldn't be sure. They moved quietly through the trees. These guys looked like they knew what they were doing—probably mercenaries or ex-military. The two pairs of men on the flanks set up on the edge of the field just inside the tree line. They were farther out than the two trip grenades. The pair on the main trail stopped at the parked explosive-laden ATV for a minute and then gave two blinks with a red filtered light. With that, the three remaining ATVs started up. As they closed in on the opening, they stared accelerating in speed. It appeared that the ATVs were going to bum-rush the cabin while the men on foot provided overwatch.

Just as the lead ATV came near the parked explosive-laden ATV, Caden touched off the charge. There was a flash explosion with a thudding echo through the trees. In the bright light of the shattered darkness, bodies flew off the first ATV, the second crashing into it and the third swerving to the right and crashing into a tree.

Staggering bodies were silhouetted by the burning ATV. Four up. Four shots. Four down. Caden looked with his night scope now on the flanks, looking for a target. He had the darkness of the trees to his advantage. He crept out onto the trail and moved silently down to where their ATVs were parked, moving into the trees to find a hiding spot to wait for the return of the others.

Caden didn't see the man crouched behind one of the ATVs. The man tried to drive his knife into Caden's chest, but he parried, sidestepped, and used the force of the thrust to pull the man off balance, elbow him in the face, and roll him to the ground in a reverse chicken wing hold. Caden drew his sidearm and shot the man in the back of the head as quickly as it began.

The man must have had time to call the others on his command headset. The four flank men were barreling toward his position now—two through the trees and two down the trail. Caden hit the remote detonation charge on the trail.

There was a brilliant flash and explosion of heat and light in the darkness of the trees. The two men rushing on the trail slammed forward on the ground. Cadet caught sight of the man on the right flank. He dove forward from the flash of heat and explosion. As soon as he was up, Caden drilled a single round through his skull. The two men on the trail were staggering to their feet now. Easy targets. Caden put them down with two shots in rapid succession.

Shooting without moving gave Caden's position away. A bullet hit the tree that Caden was tucked in behind, spraying bark and missing his head by only inches. The last man, as best as Caden could tell, was shooting from his left now. Caden dove behind the ATVs and crawled low to another position. He tossed a stick back where he had just been. Nothing. This guy was obviously smarter than the shooter from the old log shack.

Caden suspected that his next opponent also had a night scope with thermal vision mounted on his weapon. This would call for a little more caution. Caden quickly grabbed a helmet from the nearest ATV and hung it on a branch on the opposite side of the tree that shielded him. He tasseled a branch on the ground and bumped the helmet to give it movement. The shot came from about forty meters away next to a fallen tree. Caden remained motionless now, down near the ground. He moaned as if he had been shot and waited. He caught the man searching with his scope now, just a little bit higher than he should have been. *Bam!* The man flipped over while on the ground, dead as could be.

Caden crept over to the man he had just shot and took his command-and-control headset. He listened. Nothing. He then keyed the mic and whispered incoherently, listening for a response. Again, nothing. Caden judged that all targets had been neutralized. He quietly moved back up the trail, across the open field and to the cabin. Everyone was gone.

Chapter 31

COMMUNICATIONS

Caden switched on his satellite phone and waited for it to wind up and hit the available satellites. He typed in a text to establish communications. Nina was the first to acknowledge. Then Mingo. A minute later, Susan and Jake acknowledged comms.

Caden typed in "Go Voice???"

Mingo, Susan, Jake, and Nina all responded on the screen, "Roger."

Everyone switched from text to voice on their sat phones.

Caden went first, updating the group about taking out the first three targets and securing Kat and a group of scouts in the old log shed. In the second fight, nine targets went down. He returned to the cabin, and everyone was missing again. He would pick up their trail right after the communication update.

Jake went next. First, he gave an update on finding Troy and Sydney, ground-moving them to the extraction point and then moving back into position near the vehicle stables.

Mingo was up and provided his update. The protest was still going. There was one van full of soldiers moving to the vehicle stables and then moving out in multiple ATVs up the Mountain Lake trail. Mingo suspected that they were the second group that Caden fought up at the border mountain shack. He also reported that a group of ten to fifteen *soldiers* were still at the HMC housing complex.

Susan reported that she was en route to the apartment TOC after checking in Troy and Sydney into the Marquette hospital. Sydney had checked out to be okay. She was a little bruised up, but there were no fractures or concussion. The local cops had been called by the hospital, but Susan told Syd to have amnesia until they got Kat out or until the out-of-town FBI team arrived.

Finally, Nina came up on the net, clearly relieved that Caden had finally checked it. Still no FBI agents and no phone calls from agent John Anderson. For now, it looked like they were still on their own to rescue Kat. Until the FBI agents arrived, local law enforcement still couldn't be trusted. And without a warrant, their rescue mission would still be considered trespassing according to the crooked local cops. So until Kat was safe, they needed to contain the mission actions as much as they could.

Chapter 32

NO HIDING

Back at the HMC guest lodge, Dirk Astor and his goon soldiers were reviewing the playback recording showing on the computer screen. Two men in the first group of ten going up to mine shaft #5 had been wearing live-feed cameras. The team leader's video feed ended as he approached an open field. There was a shaking explosion with blinding white light and then black screen. The second camera had moved through the trees up to the edge of the open field. The explosion and flash of white blast showed from the camera at a distance of about forty yards. There were faint *pops* of a weapon with a silencer, and then the camera moved back through the trees to the trail and began rushing into the darkness. Then there was another blast with white light, the camera appearing to show a side view of the dark trail. There were a few more retorts of the silencer-mounted weapon, approaching steps in the dark, and then a booted foot coming down to crush the camera and send the computer screen into a snowy black and white fuzz.

Dirk turned to his lead goon soldier, a big muscled man with chiseled face. He looked almost silly with his man bun, but his dark cruel eyes could prevent even a hard man from laughing.

"What do you think?" Dirk Astor asked his lead goon.

The man was still studying the two screens, deep in thought, as if reading some secret encoded message.

"Whoever this is, he is good, really good. Probably ex-military… Navy Seal, Delta, or maybe an Army Ranger."

"What the fuck does that mean?" Dirk extorted, completely unimpressed. "Can you deal with this asshole or not?"

Mr. Man Bun slowly looked back at Dirk Aston. He really disliked this asshole, young Dirk Astor. The fact was, however, he was loyal to Astor money, which was much, much better than anything he earned as a traveling mercenary or freelance assassin. Not only that, but falling under the Astor *umbrella*, he was afforded protection and resources he normally wouldn't have as an international criminal.

"Yep, I can kill him," responded Dirk Astor's lead killer goon. "But I need five of my best men, two sniper rifles with night-vision scopes, a handful of automatic weapons, and some explosives. That's in addition to what we brought."

"Done," Dirk replied and nodded at one of the full-time staff members of the HMC.

At that moment, a weasel-looking guy with Coke-bottle glasses appeared from a side room.

"Mr. Astor, we finally have something!" The little weasel guy was excited with his find as he explained it to Dirk Astor.

Weasel man explained, "We had managed to isolate cell phone signals, not belonging to any of the HMC signals, and determine their sources. Two of the cell phone signals originated here on the HMC grounds and the other signal from an apartment building near the campus grounds in Marquette. Names of residents in the apartment include Callie Cartrin, Nina Orend, Caden Garrett, and Mingan Grey Wolf...people you are familiar with! We also know that the signal coming from the apartment building was from Nina Orend. Mingo Grey Wolf was one of the signals from the HMC property, the other signal was still unidentified." He continued, "Apparently, these Garrett and Grey Wolf guys were some big-deal Special Ops guys in the army."

Dirk Astor and Chisel Chin looked at each other with raised eyebrows of surprise.

"Well, that explains that," choked out Dirk Astor's lead goon soldier.

Dirk Astor's brain wheels were already turning at high speed. A few minutes passed and then a confident but cruel smile came to his face.

Young Astor looked at his lead muscle goon and started directing actions.

Bun man and five of his best men would go up to mine shaft #5 to take care of the *trespassers* up there. Dirk directed them to use the monster costume for a touch of menace and mystery to the upcoming deaths after they had killed this Special Ops guy or whatever he was. Dirk liked that special touch of the Wendigo costume because he himself had on occasion used the costume to terrorize trespassers.

Four other goon soldiers would hunt down the trespassers whose cell phone signals gave away their positions near the main activity area of the HMC.

Two other goon soldiers would go to the front gate with a dozen uniformed HMC police to quell the protest and block any traffic going in or out of the main gate. Additionally, Dirk would have the two detectives, Ryker and Shelby, get up to the main gate to ensure the protesters were "properly arrested" for rioting and trespassing.

Finally, Dirk, his silver-spoon buddies, and a couple goons would go to the apartment building near campus and pay a visit to whoever was at the end of that cell phone signal.

Chapter 33

STRIKE, PARRY, COUNTER-STRIKE

Caden followed the group's tracks behind the cabin, up the rocky trail and to the mouth of a cave. The tracks went into the cave, it seemed, with no hesitation. As he shined his light around into the maw of the cave head, he heard several AVTs coming up the mountain trail. It looked like six different bikes (ATVs) that rolled right up to the cabin and went inside. Had they been watching him?

Caden assessed that if this new group had any idea what happened to the first two groups, they would be smarter and loaded for bear—in other words, a serious threat. Caden turned on the sat phone again. He texted that he was heading into a cave system, following Kat's tracks, and would lose communications. He also texted about the new group of soldiers coming in after him and that he may need assistance. There were grenade traps to the left and right of trail near field.

The next text came from Mingo: "On the way."

Group texts popped up on Caden's sat phone screen from Jake and Nina: "Ackn."

Caden texted "Ackn," and then started working his way up the mine shaft.

Mingo moved through the trees down to where the latest group of ATVs had come from. There was a large rustic log lodge with several ATVs parked nearby. He quietly slipped down and found one with the key still in it. He quickly scanned for any bystanders, which there were none. The machine started quietly, and Mingo slowly pulled away, heading for the trail to the old cabin.

Jake had repositioned now and found a good hiding position to better observe the intersection now that Mingo had driven the ATV up the Mountain Lake trail. A pair of Range Rovers and a black sedan drove up from the main lodge area and headed out the main gate. Jake couldn't tell how many people were in the vehicles but texted the update to the group text site. "Ackn" came back on the phone screen from Nina and Susan, who was now back at the apartment. Nothing from Caden or Mingo.

Jake was enjoying breathing in the night mountain air when he noticed the slow movement in the trees. One man was walking stealthily, wearing night-vision goggles. Another leaned motionlessly against a tree, providing overwatch for the man on the move. They were covering the ground exactly where he had been set up earlier. Jake slowly scanned over to the position where Mingo had been set up. Two more men were moving with stealth, exactly where Mingo was set up. He watched for another minute.

The hair on Jake's back was now standing. These HMC soldiers were sophisticated. They had obviously pinged their cell phone locations. That meant that they probably had Susan and Nina's location too. The three vehicles that left shortly before were undoubtedly heading for their TOC, meaning Caden's apartment where Susan and Nina were waiting for the FBI agents.

Jake sent a text on the sat phone: "Three vehicles left HMC, believe heading to TOC with hostile intent. They tracked cell phones." A full minute went by without a reply. Jake waited for a response while he picked up his night scope and once again checked the progress of the four men hunting him. Finally, the response "Ackn" popped up on the screen. *It took too long*, Jake thought to himself.

Jake typed, "TOC confirm…4."

He waited a long minute, again too long. The response came back: "3."

Crap, Jake thought to himself. *The TOC with Susan and Nina was compromised.*

The correct response was 7—a number combination adding up to11.

Jake typed back, "Ackn. Switch to alt"—meaning switch to their alternate channel on the sat phone. Jake switched to the designated alternate channel on the sat phone and typed another group message: "TOC compromised. Plan Charlie Mike." When Caden and Mingo would finally come back on line, they would see a message: "Know that the TOC apartment had been compromised and to continue the mission. Updates would follow."

Jake thought out his options. He could go back to the apartment and try to intercept the intruders and rescue Susan and Nina, or he could wait in place. The *profile* of these Astor characters had been to bring their captives back to the Huron Mountain Club. That's what they would do tonight. Jake would sit tight, wait for the return of the three vehicles, and watch where they took Susan and Nina. This was really turning into a high-stakes cat-and-mouse game of "strike, parry, counter-strike." The risk now was that if FBI Agent John Anderson showed up, no one would be able to fill him in on their current operation and the location of everyone, especially the kidnap victims.

Jake turned his cell phone on. It was a risk, but he needed to let his friend FBI Agent John Anderson know where he was and what was going on. After that, Jake would need to move positions again, so he decided to start hunting the hunters.

Chapter 34

FBI AGENTS

Agent Anderson pulled his two suitcases off the airport conveyor belt. Anderson looked around at the small Michigan Upper Peninsula airport and smiled as he read the welcome sign that read, "Welcome to Sawyer International Airport." He watched as his two FBI colleagues, who had also secured two pieces of luggage apiece from the circular conveyor belt, walked toward him.

Anderson said in a low voice to his fellow agents, "I guess if they get a puddle-jumper flight from Canada in here, it would make it international."

The three big-city Detroit agents all chuckled as they went up to the rental car counter to pick up the keys for the car they reserved. While standing in the short line of two people, the three agents checked their phones.

Anderson had turned on his cell phone earlier, but just now, a message popped up. It was from Jake Catrin, the old army buddy who had convinced him that he needed to come up to Marquette because of crooked cops and kidnappings, specifically the kidnapping of Jake's girl. As John Anderson read the text, his eyebrows furrowed with growing concern.

With the car keys issued, the three men left the building and went out into the dark to find the silver Malibu in parking space F4. The rental car parking lot wasn't very big, so the car was easy to find when Anderson hit the alert button on the key fob.

Anderson would brief his team in the rental car ride from the airport to the apartment. The situation had turned more urgent now.

Jake believed that now his wife, Susan, and his nephew's girlfriend, Nina, had been forcibly taken from the apartment where they were to meet. There first stop would be the apartment to assess the situation. From there, they would pick up the search warrant for the HMC and then off to the Huron Mountain Club to serve the warrant and find the kidnapped women.

The agents followed a map quest app on a cell phone, which led them to the apartment building. The three agents found the apartment on the second floor. The door had been bashed in. The room was disheveled as if there had been a struggle. No blood, no bullet casings. At least that was a good sign. Agent Anderson tried calling Jake Catrin on his cell phone, no answer. Anderson sent a text to Jake, "Apartment broken into, women taken."

The three agents went back to their car and were off to their next stop to try to get the search warrant. Hopefully the judge wasn't corrupt too.

Chapter 35

STAND OFF

Mingo Grey Wolf had made his way up the dark trail on the ATV to within a hundred meters of the open field, crept in, and taken out the one man on sentry duty. The man lay gurgling in his own blood from the slit in his throat that cut through both of his carotid arteries. Mingo wiped the man's blood off his blade using the dying man's own shirt and then jammed the knife back into the sheath hanging from his belt. No other goon soldier sentries lurked in the trees.

Mingo hustled back to where he had set down his pack and rifle. He had dropped the bulky equipment to make the kill stalk, not wanting to alert any of the other HMC soldiers that may be nearby. He then quickly returned to the edge of the tree line.

One flick of Mingo's finger switched on the night vison of his scope. He slowly scanned the cabin and far tree-filled rock wall that climbed up to a glooming night sky. Nothing. Then Mingo turned the scope to thermal and listened as the scope went into a quiet humming and then stopped. He raised his rifle up, peering through the thermal scope at the old log cabin and then at the mountainside behind it. One man was peering out a window in the cabin, and it looked like two or three men moving within the rocks about forty meters up the side of the mountain. Mingo watched and listened for another ten minutes, scanning the tree line, the woods behind him, the rocky outcropping, and then back again to the cabin and mountainside. Still only one in the cabin, three on the side of the mountain.

Settling into a good, comfortable, prone position on the ground, Mingo lay concealed, waiting for the right opportunity to take out the solo man in the cabin. Another fifteen minutes went by, no change. One thermal image in the cabin, still three thermal images on the side of the mountain. Mingo lay perfectly still and waited.

The explosion on the side of the mountain slapped Mingo out of his random thoughts. His eyes had been fixed on the cabin still standing subdued in the darkness of the night, but his mind had been wandering. Mingo shifted to look with his thermos scope at the side of the mountain from where the explosion occurred. There appeared to be warm body parts scattered around. To the left and right of the pieces of flesh that had just moments before been a living human being, two currently living bodies appeared to be scrambling around to find protection among the boulders.

A few long seconds after the blast, the single man from the cabin came stumbling out, ran to the side of the cabin, and began searching the side of the mountain with what looked like a pair of binoculars. This was the moment Mingo was waiting for. He settled the crosshairs on the back of the man's head and squeezed the trigger. The 7.62-round splattered the back of the man's head into mist and goo as his knees buckled and he dropped to the ground. Mingo shifted now, trying to pick out a target on the side of the mountain. One thermal image of a man dove to a new hiding position to block a shot from Mingo. The other man dashed for a different boulder but wasn't quite quick enough. Mingo touched off another shot, hitting the man in a trailing leg. Mingo tightened his body, focused, and got ready for the next shot.

The shot came from the rock outcropping about halfway up. Mingo's rifle, along with the night-vision scope, seemed to kick away, splintering and shattering into a hundred broken pieces. Somehow Mingo had missed spying the sniper up in the rock outcropping to his right. Mingo tucked in tight behind a tree to avoid getting whacked by this new sniper threat. His face was bleeding but not bad. Both his eyes were still good to go. He needed to back away from the field opening and get into the cover of the trees. All Mingo had remaining now was his knife, a 9mm pistol, his light pack, and his wit. Oh, and the two grenade booby traps Caden had set earlier.

Mingo fired two shots with his 9mm up toward the rocky outcropping. He then backed away, keeping a large spruce tree in the line of sight between him and the hidden sniper. Once he was well into the tree line and out of sight of any thermal sniper scope, he moved quickly to where several ATVs sat and one body lay lifeless on the ground—some of Caden's handiwork from earlier. He quickly pulled a spark plug cap from one of the bikes (ATVs) and pressed the electric start. The motor turned over and over and over again but did not start. Mingo stopped and listened. Nothing. He jumped on the seat now, jamming down on the manual kick start, and cursed loudly. He stopped again to listen. This time, he heard rocks rolling and steps sliding as the sniper hurried down the rocky outcropping.

Mingo quickly replaced the spark plug cap, hit the electric start, revved the machine, and then ducked into the darkness to wait on the sniper.

The man was on a dead run now, quickly crossing the field to the trail that headed into the dark woods and back to the main compound of HMC. He ran about ten meters into the wood line and then found a tree to stabilize his shot at the fleeing ATV. He switched his thermals back to the *on* position of his scope. The sniper only saw heat from a running ATV engine. It would be the last thing he saw as Mingo's 9mm's quick report sent a bullet slamming into the sniper's head.

Mingo stepped over to the man's still twitching body and picked up the sniper's rifle. *Nice*, Mingo thought to himself as he examined the weapon. He then stripped the man of his extra three ten-round magazines and worked his way to the edge of the wood line. The thermal switch was still in the *on* position with the scope as Mingo spied the cabin, the mountainside, and the surrounding area. Nothing picked up with the thermals.

Mingo decided to chance it and made a quick dash to the old log storage shed. Inside, there were no bodies, no people. Only three pair of shackles on the floor and an assortment of dusty old workshop items and the smell that someone had been smoking. Mingo slid to the back window, which was now slid open, and used the scope to recon up the mountainside. Standing off to the side of the window to avoid making himself a target, he carefully glassed the boulders and trees. Still no tell-tale thermal image of anything resembling a living creature, only the quickly fading heat signature of body parts of the man who had been blown apart by Caden's M203 round.

Caden was in a stand-off now with the HMC soldiers working their way out of mine shaft #5. Caden had seen the sign that read "HMC Mine Shaft #5," and Randy had shown him where the other mine shaft was. Randy also told Caden about the side cave they had come in from, down below, from the McCormick Wilderness Area. Caden was gaining a better appreciation of this group of Adventure Bound Scouts, what they were doing, and their skill set.

Still, thought Caden, *these were a bunch of kids and civilians, and they were up against some trained professional killers. No place or time to risk their lives, if he could help it.*

Caden and the HMC soldiers had exchanged gunfire in the shaft, Caden always drawing fire and returning it, trying to get them in a position to take them out with a HE203 round. The shot at the mine shaft entrance had taken one out, he thought, but the next two had bounced down the cave shaft well beyond the intended targets and detonated, barely causing a ringing ear. Caden was down to his last 203 round, his last magazine of 5.56, and his 9mm sidearm with twenty-eight rounds. The weapons they had scavenged off the dead bodies below only had a handful of rounds. Still, it might be enough to put together a workable plan, which Caden set into motion.

The lead goon, Chisel Jaw, and three other soldiers were now working their way up mine shaft #5 to the opening at the top. The near miss with the first M203 round had been too close and cost them one man. They were all wearing thermal-vision goggles now and using small smoke grenades to conceal their movement. They were pushing forward a little at a time and making their opponent use up his ammo. The standoff would soon be over, and they were moving in for the kill. They had this guy outgunned, and it was just a matter of time now. Chisel Jaw smiled to himself. He could taste blood now, and he relished the thrill of the kill, especially human kill.

Two of the HMC soldiers slowly crawled low up to just inside the mine shaft #5 opening, remaining out of sight. They scanned with their night-vision goggles for any thermal images. Nothing. A man crouched forward from the #5 shaft opening, moving between the two prone soldiers and stepping out just enough to project his silhouette to an outside observer. Three shots came from across the small open field and the other open mine shaft, none connecting with flesh. Both men lying in the prone position fired rapidly into the dark opening of the other shaft. Two smoke grenades spit forward out into the small opening and from shaft #5 and the HMC soldiers. As soon as the smoke started spewing thick clouds of smoke into the dark air, the two men in prone position rushed out, moving to each flank of the opposing mine shaft opening. From inside shaft #5, rapid firing continued toward the opposing shaft through the thick smoke.

Caden sat perched above shaft #5, tucked in behind a boulder, and waiting for the rush of soldiers from inside the shaft. He watched as the two smoke grenades were tossed out, fizz popped, and started clouding the opening. Caden watched as two men rush forward, heading to the flanks as automatic rifle fire covered their move. Caden's first shot hit the man on the right square in the back as he flopped forward, wriggling wildly. Caden adjusted quickly and snapped off the second shot at the man rushing away on the left and dove into the smoke screen. He wasn't sure if he hit that target. On all accounts, Caden thought the sound of his shots were concealed by the automatic rifle fire of the HMC soldiers. He quickly shifted positions to get a better shot at the man on the left—that is, in case he missed him—and prepare for the next rush of men from the shaft #5 opening.

The next thing that came out of the mine shaft opening stunned even Caden. It was a giant figure covered in matted hair and with a dog-looking face and a great set of antlers mounted on its head. Caden blinked hard to clear his vision. The monster now arched its terrible head back and bellowed out a bloodcurdling half scream, half roar that sent chills up and down Caden's spine.

"What the f— a Wendigo?!" Caden was thinking to himself as this *monster* matched Mingo's description of a Wendigo as it emerged from the shaft and let out its bloodcurdling scream. Caden was still staring at this thing when he felt the slam against the back of his head, saw stars, slumped forward on a boulder, and then plunged the ten feet to the ground in a resounding thud.

One of the mine shaft occupants had flanked Caden while he was distracted by the screaming Wendigo creature. The man had bashed Caden in the side of the head with a rock and was now working his way back down the slope to finish the head bashing.

Caden was still stunned and seeing stars, trying to gain control of his senses, when the man jumped the last three feet to the ground. The Wendigo creature had vanished into the smoke and was heading to the other shaft entrance where Kat and the Adventure Bound Scouts were hiding. An ironic smile came to Caden's face as he thought about the adventure these boys were having now.

Move! the voice in Caden's head screamed as the heavy boot came smashing down with hostile intent. Caden rolled, the boot just missing his head. Caden scrambled and then staggered to his feet. There was no one else in sight except this one opponent now, who was wielding an eight-inch SOF-style fighting knife and a confident, cruel face.

Caden's vision still hadn't fully returned as he tried to focus on the task at hand. The man drove the knife forward, nearly missing as Caden sidestepped, parried, and wheeled with a back-elbow strike to the man's head. Caden was operating on muscle memory and reflex now. Caden's opponent went down, rolling, and was right back on his feet again. The hand-to-hand combat went back and forth now with neither man gaining the advantage. The smoke grenade cloud was clearing now, and Caden remained wary of a return of the monster and the other flanking shooter. One man lay still on the ground, but clearly the other shooter was gone.

Finally, Caden was able to completely regain his senses, disarm his opponent, and use the man's knife against him to end the fight with the SOF-style knife handle protruding from the assailant's temple.

Caden was breathing hard now, his head throbbing from the rock to the head. He was looking back toward the opening of shaft #5, thinking he saw movement. The click from behind him was unmistakable—a safety selector switch on an M-4 rifle. Caden twisted to see the source or the sound just as the shooter was raising his rifle to his shoulder, pointing at Caden with deadly intent. Caden tried to duck, but the shooter was quick, and a double shot penetrated the night mountain air. The stinging heat was unmistakable. He had been shot before in combat and had been familiar with the feeling. Caden went down, now rolling, to avoid being a sitting duck target. He dove for the cover of a nearest boulder and noticed out of the corner of his eye that the shooter was now only a pile on the ground.

Mingo's voice came from inside shaft #5, and he stepped out in the open. Mingo had arrived just in time, killing the goon soldier just as he was about to blow out Caden's brains. It wasn't the first time Mingo saved Caden's life, and it probably wouldn't be the last.

Caden blinked, trying to clear his vision. There was now blood trickling into an eye from the grazing shot to the head. Caden had been lucky, and he knew it.

Mingo moved up to Caden. "You all right?" Mingo could see the blood but not the wound.

"Ya, I'm fine," replied Caden. "It's just a scratch."

The two ducked into the protection of some nearby boulders where Mingo patched up Caden's *scratch*. Caden got Mingo up to speed on Kat, the scout troop, and the Wendigo monster that apparently Mingo had just missed seeing.

Mingo looked at Caden with a questioning look on his face, not sure whether Caden was joking or not.

"A Wendigo?" Mingo asked. "You are kidding, right?"

Canden shook his head no, describing the beast to a still disbelieving Mingo.

"What didn't make sense was why it was here with the HMC soldiers so close by and coming from mine shaft #5," said Caden, thinking out loud to Mingo.

"It was probably one of them in some type of costume," Mingo said, "as a trick to get the jump on you, which they did."

Caden nodded in concurrence to his best friend Mingo, who was just finishing up the Band-Aid job on Caden's head.

They would need to assess their options and get after Kat and the scouts to get them back to safety. If they could, they would also figure out exactly who this Wendigo character really was.

Chapter 36

FIGHTING BACK

Jake had just finished taking out the two HMC soldiers who were searching around the vehicle motor stables. Two quick shots with his silencer-mounted 9mm dropped the two men, each like a sack of rocks. Earlier, Jake had worked in on each of the two sentry soldiers searching Mingo's old outlook position. They had been creeping along through the trees, and Jake had managed to use the darkness and trees to get the drop on them, breaking one man's neck and knifing the other while muffling his attempts to scream.

By this time, the protesters at the front gate had been subdued. The pair of HMC goons had started by beating up the protest leaders as the two cops, Ryker and Shelby, started having rioters and trespassers arrested and carted off to waiting police vans.

Jake sent a sitrep to the group channel on the sat phone text screen. No response from anyone. He then took out the cell phone and turned it on. A text popped up from his friend, FBI Agent John Anderson.

The text told Jake several things. First, the agents had arrived and gone to the apartment. Susan and Nina were not there and were probably taken after a struggle. No blood, so it didn't look like anyone was injured. Additionally, the agents had the search warrant for HMC and were on their way, not far behind the Astor vehicles.

It was now time to unleash the "dogs of war," Jake thought to himself. He looked up from the text just in time to see the three vehicles coming up the road from the main gate of the HMC. All three vehicles were moving fast as they made the corner heading to the main lodging area. The lead vehicle was a silver Land Rover, the second a luxury black sedan, the third another silver Land Rover.

"Bingo," Jake said to himself as he set the frequency of his remote detonator to the charge Mingo had planted by the road going to the main lodging area. Jake flipped up the safety switch and pressed the red button. The bright explosion sent the lead Land Rover into a side spin, rolling over on its side and blocking the road to the lodges.

The trailing black sedan and second Rover stopped and quickly backed the vehicles to the maintenance vehicle parking stables. Men were crawling out of the flipped Rover now and shooting aimlessly into the dark. Jake picked his targets with his night-scoped rifle and thwacked two of the would-be assailants back into the disabled Rover.

Over at the vehicle stables, armed men were piling out of the second Rover, shooting in Jake's direction and beginning to maneuver in his direction. Four people got out of the black sedan, forcing at least one woman out and into the Rover. Jake watched the vehicle transfer and popped off two men trying to maneuver to his left flank.

The mobile Land Rover with one, maybe two, women spun out and headed up the Mountain Lake trail. Two other HMC soldiers were now trying to maneuver to flank Jake from the right. Jake switched the detonator frequency to the charge he had set in the ditch by the intersection leading to the vehicle stables. He then flipped up the safety bar and pressed the detonation button, setting off the charge. There was a simultaneous explosion and bright flash of light in the darkness. One man was sent cartwheeled through the air, landing lifelessly on the intersection. The two soldiers maneuvering to the right of Jake were temporarily blinded by the explosion, frozen in place, momentarily looking for cover. That was all the time Jake needed as he dispatched the two with a quick pair of successive shots. Jake ran back deeper into the trees to reposition himself to better handle the two snipers that ran into the old shed and the two men who were ducked behind the sedan.

Jake set the detonator frequency to that of the charge set on the old shed. This was the last of Jake and Mingo's preset charges. Jake thought to himself that this would be enough. Jake watched through his thermal scope as the two snipers set themselves up back in the shadows of the old shed. They would probably have thermal scopes on their rifles, so Jake couldn't wait too long. Jake pressed the button on the remote and shielded his eyes from the bright flash of the explosion. One man dove out from behind the black sedan, and Jake settled the scope's crosshairs and touched off a round, slumping the man over, lifeless in the dirt. Another man, completely engulfed in flames, burst out of the now burning building. Jake collapsed the man while the guy was mid-stride, sending his still burning body to the ground.

Flame on, buddy! Jake thought to himself.

A bullet hit the tree Jake was using for cover. The shot came from a gunman crouched behind the sedan. Jake moved quickly again back deeper into the trees. Jake was thinking now that this guy probably had a thermal scope mounted on his rifle.

Within the safety of the trees, Jake heard another gunfire. It was coming from the direction of the HMC main gate. One shot, then another, then a succession of shots. *That had to be John Anderson trying to serve the search warrant*, Jake thought to himself. Jake hoped he hadn't brought his friend into a death trap.

Jake waited, watching and listening. Finally, he heard a vehicle coming up the road from the main gate entrance. Jake moved quickly forward, keeping a tree in the line of sight between him and the black sedan. A silver sedan was coming up the road now, heading toward the intersection of the motor stable, the main lodge complex, and the trail heading to Mountain Lake. The shooter had repositioned from the black sedan to the edge of the main parking structure and shot once at the oncoming silver sedan. Jake saw the shooter now, settled the crosshairs, and squeezed. The shot sent the HMC soldier into a death clump on the ground. The silver sedan came to a stop on the main road.

Jake rushed down to the silver sedan to find his friend John Anderson sitting in the front passenger seat and bleeding from a gunshot wound to the shoulder. The agent in the back seat had a pistol raised and pointed at Jake Catrin, uncertain whether he was friendly or enemy. So far, this hadn't been a real warm welcome to Marquette and the Huron Mountain Club for these FBI agents. The agent who had been driving wasn't faring so well. He had been shot in the chest by the sniper and was now leaned over the steering wheel dead.

Jake told the agent in the back seat his name and said he was a friend of John Anderson and then pulled the car door and started to apply first aid on his friend who now was slipping in an out of consciousness. Before passing out, Agent Anderson told Jake that the state police and the local sheriff were on their way.

The agent from the back seat was now out and pulled the dead agent from behind the steering wheel of the rental car. The sniper's bullet had pierced the front windshield before finding its mark on the FBI agent driving the car.

As Jake worked first aid on his friend, the remaining conscious FBI agent suddenly whispered loudly, pointing in the direction of the black sedan, "Who is that?"

Jake looked up the road and toward the car garage where the black sedan was parked. There walking up toward them was a woman walking slowly with unsteady steps. He recognized the figure in the murky dark immediately; it was his wife, Susan.

Chapter 37

LEGEND

Caden and Mingo were now moving quickly down the cave tunnel, which branched off to the left from the main mine shaft. Mingo halted, shining his flashlight at the ancient scribing on the cave walls.

"Caden, look at this!" Mingo whispered loudly to his best friend, who was already a good ten steps ahead and heading in the downslope of the ancient hole in the rock.

Caden worked his way back to Mingo, who was now looking closely at the ancient drawings on the rock wall and lightly tracing the images with his fingers, as if to *feel* the meaning of the scribing.

The two brothers-in-arms were now both looking at the cave drawings with some fascination while keeping an attentive ear down the shaft from the direction the drops of blood were leading.

"What do you think?" asked Caden, who was now looking at the primitive drawing of the great antlered beast who was fighting the group of sticklike figures etched around it.

"I've seen these before," Mingo replied after a long pause of careful examination. "Not exactly these drawings but drawings in the dirt similar to this when the elders were telling us as kids the legends of the Wendigo."

Caden looked at Mingo, half-expecting that old familiar smile after telling a subtle joke. There was no jokester's smile, only a serious furrowed brow on a serious and sober face. Mingo looked back at Caden.

"What did you see out there?" Mingo questioned Caden.

Caden went on to explain the similarities between the etching on the wall and the monster he briefly saw. Caden explained again how the creature howled and then disappeared into the cloud of smoke just before he took a blow to the head. Mingo watched his friend talk, trying to judge whether what Caden saw was fake or maybe an illusion. This was getting more interesting and dangerous by the minute, or so it seemed.

Finally, Mingo said, "Well, whatever this creature is, Wendigo or no Wendigo, we need to get back on the trail and find Kat. That's our mission."

Caden nodded in concurrence. "Right, let's get going."

The two were off again, following the scuffing trail of Kat, the Adventure Bound Scouts, and the creature.

The cave had narrowed somewhat but continued in a downslope, finally coming to a ledge and an abrupt drop where a climbing rope was still tied off and hanging to the ground. Caden and Mingo stopped at the ledge top and listened. They could hear the rustling of feet running through the underbrush and hear the boyish scream of obvious terror.

Caden and Mingo were down the rope in a heartbeat.

Caden called out loudly, "Over here!" hoping to draw the attention of the scrambled troop, Kat included, and the beast. Mingo set up in a concealed position, ready for a shot if the beast were to come out. Mingo also was to cover their withdrawal back up the chimney climb to the ledge from where the rope still dangled.

Kat was the first to emerge from the trees that were still immersed in darkness. "Something is after us!" she cried out as she saw Caden.

"I know! Climb back up the rope, we are going to get everyone out of here!" Caden ordered her. "Help with the others at the top as they come up!"

Caden kept calling as he heard the hurried rustling of feet in darkness. One by one, the scouts started appearing from out of the darkness and trees. Five boys now had appeared and were sent up the rope. Randy Adams, one of the adult scout leaders, was next to make it out of the trees. He was bleeding from what looked like three parallel cuts across his upper arm.

"What the hell is that?" Randy whispered loudly to Caden as he emerged from the darkness and closed the distance to where Caden was standing and still calling out.

"I think we are going to find out soon!" Caden whispered back urgently. "Where is Reggie?"

"I don't know," Randy replied. "We lost him in the dark when that *thing* caught up to us in the trees."

Caden told Randy to climb back up the rope, take the boys and Kat back to the first mine shaft opening by the old cabin, and wait for him and his friend Mingo, who had now joined the fight. Caden and Mingo would deal with this *thing*, as Reggie called it, and find the rest of the boys and meet them.

"It will be light in a few hours," Caden explained. "Try to make cell phone contact with your base camp from the top of the mountain and tell them to send assistance from the state police and the FBI, *not* the local police." Randy gave Caden a puzzled look after his last comment.

"We think there might be some local crooked cops working with some of the shadier characters of the Huron Mountain Club," replied Caden in response to Randy's quizzical look. With that, Randy was over to the rope and scaling up the cliff.

The screams of the boy were muffled and close as Caden looked into the darkness in the direction of the source. There was the hurried and panicked rustling of feet.

"Over here!" Caden yelled.

The boy was in a panic and at a dead run for Caden. Caden grabbed the boy and led him to the rope.

"Climb now!" Caden demanded.

One shot rang out in the darkness, then two more. Caden swirled in time to see the beast jerk back and then twist, jerking back two more times at Mingo's three shots to its body. The beast went down, wriggling, paused, and then was back on its feet.

The beast's roaring scream was the same as Caden had heard up on the top of the mountain, and the same chills ran down his spine as he reacted by bringing his weapon up into a firing position. Caden shot the beast three times in the chest, and he heard another two shots coming from Mingo's hidden position. Again, the beast jerked and writhed, but this time, it remained standing on its two hind legs.

The beast now moved quickly toward Caden, much quicker than Caden thought possible. The beast was belching out a guttural growl now and took a great swipe at Caden, severing the sling that held Caden's M-4. Caden wasn't sure how he avoided being slashed by the great beast, but he wasn't going to stand still and give it another free swing. Two more shots came from Mingo, again hitting the creature.

Caden rolled away from the beast, pulling his knife from the scabbard. Mingo shot two more times, striking the beast in the chest. Caden dove forward, narrowly missing another deadly swipe of the beast's clawed arm. Caden rolled again but now forward toward the creature and this time severing the beast's Achilles tendon with his blade. The beast bellowed out in pain, dropping to one knee.

Mingo shot three more times, all aimed at the beast's body, giving Caden the chance to spring upon the beast's back and drive his knife deep into the base of its skull. This time, the great beast went down, fighting its impending death and reaching back as if to claw Caden and free itself from the blade.

Caden had already jumped back out of range of the clawing beast. Mingo now rushed forward and delivered a final killing shot to the brain of the Wendigo.

Caden and Mingo both stood there looking at each other, half-expecting the *thing* to get up again. The beast appeared to be dead as a doornail.

A weak, squeaky voice came from the base of the cliff by the rope. There still standing was the last scout the beast had been chasing. He was obviously shaken up and, based on the smell, had clearly shit his pants.

"What is it?" croaked out the boy.

"We think it's a Wendigo," Mingo said softly, trying to calm the scout.

The boy only had a puzzled look on his face, obviously never having heard of a Wendigo.

Randy was now coming down the rope, his headlamp light bouncing off the face of the cliff. One by one, all the scouts came down the rope, including Kat, to get a closer look at the creature.

The creature appeared to be large, covered in matted fur and with a wolflike face and long muscled arms with deadly claws protruding from long fingers. There were whispers back and forth, everyone not really sure if what they were seeing was even real. All the LED lights were focused on the creature's monstrous head, face, and antlers. Finally, one of the braver scouts pushed on one of the antlers as if touching it would confirm what they were seeing. The body of the beast reacted with a release of air that had all the boys scrambling away in terror.

Mingo and Caden chuckled and continued scanning the body with their flashlights. Caden had picked up his weapon with the cut sling that had been cut by the beast. Caden looked at the clean cut on the sling and then examined the claws of the creature. Sharp, very sharp, too sharp. Caden worked down the creature's furry body to the feet. Something was *off*. Caden lifted one of the heavy feet, and a flap of furry hide slid to the side, exposing a thick soled boot. Under the matted fur of the chest area was lightweight body armor, which explained how it could take being shot in the body. Mingo and Caden looked at each other again, now with the group of boys starting to return.

Mingo took a hold of one of the antlers; the texture was more of a rubbery material. Pulling hard, he could feel the head covering loosen up. Now he grabbed both antlers and pulled. The head covering was being held by a chin strap. He worked the mask off and exposed a tough-looking, chiseled face with several scars. This was no Wendigo; it was a man! Probably from the same group that they had been fighting. Kat, the scouts, and Randy Adams all stood there staring in shock at the discovery.

Chapter 38

DEADLY RECKONING

Dirk Astor was in the back seat of the Land Rover, smirking at Nina Orend, who was leaning away and bound by the wrists and ankles with thick tape. She had attempted to headbutt and then kick Dirk Astor as he stroked her hair. Nina would have spit at the guy except for the fact that her mouth was taped over too.

"You are going to be one fine piece of ass, baby!" Dirk reassured her as the driver of the Land Rover slowly worked the way up the tight trail leading to the old cabin at the outer boarder of the Huron Mountain Club.

Dirk and his boys had surprised Susan Catrin and Nina Orend in the Marquette apartment building. It wasn't hard to find them from the cell phone signal and the names on the apartments. Dirk was hoping to kill Caden Garrett and Mingan Grey Wolf in their apartment, but instead, they got a bonus prize of two lovely women. The older woman Dirk was going to leave down below as a toy for his security detail. This younger one, however, was grade AAA pussy, and he would have first dibs.

The explosion earlier down by the main road going into the lodging area was only a minor setback. Dirk had a plan for everything, and this was no different. The fact that this was a little bit of a challenge just made the game that much more fun. Dirk had deduced correctly that Caden Garrett and Mingan Grey Wolf were the ones causing trouble, *trespassing* on the HMC grounds. They were being dealt with even as the Rover worked the trail up the mountain. If the two ex-Army flunkies were still alive, which Dirk doubted, he would make them watch as he fucked this gorgeous morsel and did all kinds of kinky things with her. Then he would kill them. If they were already dead…well, it didn't really matter.

Finally, the silver Range Rover made it to the high mountain clearing and the old log storage shed. It pulled up to the front door of the cabin and stopped. Dirk told the goon sitting in the front passenger seat to call the top henchman, Chevnay Ridgeman, the chisel-faced mercenary, and see where they were. There was no signal on the cell phone.

"Check in on the sat phone then, dumbass," Dirk said impatiently.

Still nothing. Dirk told the two thugs in the front to get out and check the area out. Meanwhile, he would do a line of coke…and get in the mood. The men went around the back of the Range Rover, opened it, and searched through the small inventory of weapons. Finally, they each pulled out an assault-style automatic weapon and a pair of night-vision goggles.

Dirk had flipped down a custom airline-style lap table from the back of the front seat. He drew out a line of cocaine and snorted it. He felt the immediate rush. He then turned to Nina, smiling.

"Better than Viagra, sweetheart. Get ready for date night, baby!" Dirk said as he chuckled at his own sense of humor and then watched the men outside doing their security check.

Outside the Range Rover, the two men, clad with rifles and night-vision goggles, checked the inside of the cabin, then around the sides, and then to the back. Nothing unusual so far. One of the men walked up to Dirk's window, which he powered down halfway.

"We are going to check out the perimeter, Dirk," said the New York thug, who then flipped the night-vision goggles back down and headed to the rock outcropping. The second man of Dirk's security detail was already heading to the tree line, back in the direction of the mountain trail and the litter of parked or broken ATVs.

The second gunman walked the tree line, whacked his shin on a broken branch, and cursed. The night-vision googles were good for general sight at night but cut off peripheral vision downward when walking and looking forward. It would be light in about an hour, and he would be glad to take these things off. He kept working his way along into the tree line but tried to move a little more cautiously now. The man felt the slight pressure on his shin, heard the slight metallic noise, and realized too late what he had just run into. It wasn't another tree limb to whack his shin; it was a trip wire.

The other New York thug gunman was working his way up the rocky outcropping and dove to the ground when the grenade exploded across the field. He heard the other man screaming in pain for a minute, and then there was silence. Lying on the ground up on the rock outcropping, he had a good overview of the field, the tree line, and the cabin where the Land Rover was parked, still containing that little prick, Dirk Astor. He would sit tight for a little bit to see what would unfold next.

The man on the rocky outcropping waited a full ten minutes. Everything remained quite except for the smell of explosive and burned flesh in the air, and that seemed to have a sickly quietness about it too. The man was still wondering if he should move his position. The asshole in the car, Dirk Astor, was probably knocking out a piece of ass right now—that is, if he hadn't shit his pants from the explosion.

Inside the Rover, Dirk was trying to get the pants off Nina, and she was fighting back hard. Dirk was getting really pissed now because she had kicked him in the balls once he freed her legs. It was just then that the explosion wilted his intentions. Even Nina stopped fighting now, waiting for the inevitable—Caden coming to the rescue. But he didn't. Nothing but silence followed the explosion. Both remained perfectly still, waiting for the inevitable next thing to happen…but it didn't.

Ten minutes passed and then Dirk Astor decided to buckle his pants back up and go outside to see where those incompetent dickheads were. Dirk went to the back of the Rover, popped open the back, and pulled out a rifle, a pistol, and a flashlight. The pistol he tucked in his waistline in the center of his back. He quickly examined the semi-automatic AK-47, chambered a round, and then started walking toward the cabin. The young Astor stopped cold when he heard the sound of small rocks being pushed by footsteps. Someone was coming down the side of the mountain from the direction of mine shaft #5. Behind him, one of his security goons was coming from the rocky outcropping. There was no sign of the second New York thug.

The security goon stopped short of Dirk and started to tell him that he had seen nothing after the explosion and that the other man was MIA…missing. The man only blurted out a few words when Dirk held up his hand and gave a quick retort "Shhh!" The man stopped and joined Dirk Astor in listening into the darkness of the mountainside.

The form worked its way from the mine shaft opening and then down to the backside of the old cabin.

Dirk Astor and his one remaining security guard had moved to the back side of the cabin to get a better look at what was coming and to conceal themselves in the shadows.

Whatever or whoever was coming down from the mine shaft opening was getting closer now and starting to take form. That form was massive, towering above the two men. Large antlers topped the creature's head. Salivating drool streamed from the jowls of the wolf-like face. Long muscled arms wore talon-like, sharp, claw-tipped fingers. The guttural growl that came from the massive dark form seemed to hold only menace and death.

Dirk was unimpressed. "Okay, Ridgeman you asshole, did you get them?"

For the moment, the creature stood still with glowing yellow eyes, contemplating.

The security guy had become unnerved at the first sight of the creature, but with Dirk's new attitude, he figured this *thing* was just Chevney Ridgeman in that goofy werewolf costume.

"Damn, Chev, you scared the shit out of me," the man said to the huge form that he assumed was the lead security man, Chevney Ridgeman, as he started to laugh out loud.

The laugh, however, was cut short by the swatting rake of the beast's giant claw. The security man was whipped to the ground like a rag doll.

The Wendigo had closed the distance between them, much quicker than the men could react.

"What the fuck are you doing!" yelled Dirk, completely unimpressed that this creature could be anything other than his ranking security man, Chevney Ridgeman.

Undeterred, the Wendigo leapt upon the downed security man in one gore-filled flash of death. Its great jaws clamped on the man's head as it tore off one of the security goon's arms. The poor man was now screaming in pain as blood spurted out the torn stump. The man's life now was pumping out in messy red spurts.

Maybe it was the man's screams. Maybe it was the flying blood and gore that splattered on the ground. Or maybe it was the pure carnage and viciousness of the attack. It had finally hit Dirk Astor that maybe, just maybe, this wasn't his head security man Chevney Ridgeman.

Dirk raised his AK-47 and fired a volley of 7.62 rounds into the creature and watched in horror as they had little to no effect on it. The tearing of flesh and limb continued even as Dirk emptied his magazine into the creature.

This was enough, however, to get the creature to shift focus and attention toward Dirk.

Dirk was wasting no time reloading; he didn't have a second magazine, and now with the hate-filled reddish, yellow eyes glaring at him, he forgot all about the pistol tucked in his belt. The Wendigo slowly stood with blood, guts, and torn flesh dripping from its jowls; now it was razor-focused on Dirk Astor.

Dirk sprinted around the old cabin, making a beeline for the parked Land Rover. Inside the vehicle, the windows were partially steamed over from the exertion of Nina working to free herself from the remaining wrist ties and gag of tape. Nina saw Dirk Astor sprinting around the corner of the cabin and managed to lock all the doors just in time. Dirk grabbed a door handle and tried to pull it open, but it was locked.

"Open the fucking door, you cunt!" he screamed as he looked back in the direction he had just come.

Nina stuck her middle finger up at him in defiance. It was then that Dirk remembered he still had the pistol and he pulled it out, pointing it at the window.

It was at that very moment a guttural screaming howl of the Wendigo shot through Dirk Astor's being as if stung into a state of paralysis. Nina heard the howling scream through the shield of the vehicle's shell but could barely make out the looming giant figure through the steamed glass.

The beast's terrible scream had stopped, and now Dirk was at a dead run across the field, heading toward the trail and the few operational ATVs that remained.

*****

At the mouth of mine shaft #5, Caden, Mingo, Kat, and the Adventure Bound Scouts had just cleared the opening and were looking down to the cabin through the boulders, trees, and fading darkness. The guttural screaming howl cut through the night air like a dull knife cutting into flesh. It was edgy, cruel, and sickening all at the same time.

The group had managed to round up all the scouts, build a makeshift litter for Reggie Townsend, and get them out of the mine shaft system and back to the mouth of mine shaft #5 above the cabin. They had made cell phone contact with the scout base camp where Amanda Adams, in turn, contacted medical emergency services and the state police. A medivac helicopter from the hospital in Marquette would be arriving shortly after daylight in the field in front of the old cabin. State police, FBI, and search teams were also on their way.

As the group watched with cautious fascination down toward the old cabin, they could make out the image of a man sprinting across the open field, away from the old cabin and toward where the ATVs were parked. The sprinting man was about halfway across the field when they saw a large figure lumbering after the man and gaining on him. The race continued into the tree line, just to the left of where the recreational ATVs were littered about.

Caden and Mingo motioned for the group to follow as they quickly began to descend to the cabin. Suddenly, the stillness of the rescinding night was shattered with the explosion of the last of Caden's booby trap hand grenades. Caden and Mingo urged the group to keep moving despite the explosion. Caden wanted them all in the cabin by daylight so they could get ready for the medevac flight. Inside the cabin would also be a good location for Caden and Mingo to keep a close eye on everyone and protect them if needed.

Mingo and Caden came around the front of the cabin, Mingo going into the building first to make sure it was clear. Caden saw the Land Rover and signaled to Mingo that he would check the vehicle out. Like a line of little ducklings, the scout troop and Kat followed Mingo into the building when he signaled for them to come in.

Nina was freed of all her binding now and was lying flat on the back seat, trying to stay out of sight. She heard the explosion, the rustling of feet, and quiet whispers but wasn't sure if it was part of Dirk Astor's crew or the large form she had seen. She almost melted when she saw the face peering into the window. It was Caden.

The back door of the Rover flung open, and Nina wrapped around Caden in a big tear-filled hug.

"Babe, are you okay?" Caden asked as he looked at her face and gave her a once-over.

"Yes, but—" started Nina, but Caden cut her short.

"We have to get in the cabin now, this isn't over yet!" Caden said, trying to impress urgency and calm at the same time.

"Caden!" yelled Mingo through the open door. "Quick…now!"

The beast was moving like a freight train, barreling down on Caden and coming from across the field. It was coming on all fours and moving fast—too fast.

"Nina…now…go!" Caden yelled at Nina, this time with no sense of calm, only urgency that sent her sprinting toward the cabin door. There was no way they would make it as fast as this thing was moving. Caden sprinted forward to meet the charge, Mingo leaping out of the cabin door to the hood of the Land Rover to get a stable shot.

The antlered demon radiated pure hate from its reddish yellow eyes. Sharp claws were tearing up clods of dirt as it moved unearthly fast with a four-legged galloping charge.

Mingo took the first shot, aiming for the head. The beast only shook it off and was almost on Caden; Nina was just inside the cabin door now. As if in slow motion, the beast took one final lunge as if going for the kill on Caden. Mingo shot again, and Caden launched forward and then slid under the beast feet first.

The Wendigo had completely missed Caden as it sailed through the air, clutching and gnashing where Caden should have been. It had crashed onto the ground, but seeing the door still partially open and another prey target, it charged the door. Randy and Kat had managed to slam the door closed and locked. Caden was now up and firing rounds into the creature's spine and back of the head. Mingo, too, had swung around and was dumping more lead into the beast.

Nina was now safely inside the locked cabin. The time and distance between life and death with this beast was only a fraction of a second. Its speed, strength, and agility were not human at all. Caden and Mingo were now convinced this was not some man wearing a costume.

Caden and Mingo had saved Nina, but now they were exposed to all the wrath of this beast. The Land Rover might serve as a temporary barrier, but eventually it would be one on one. For now, their strength was working as a team, as they usually did. Divide the creature's attention until they could figure out its weakness, if it had any. Right now, though, this looked like a really tough fight.

Caden and Mingo moved to put the vehicle between themselves and the ravaging creature and kept some distance between themselves. The Wendigo charged again, this time going for Mingo; Caden shot twice, hitting it both times; and Mingo averted the slashing of claws only by speed and luck.

To the surprise of the two ex-Army ranger gladiators, a shot rang out from the cabin window. It was Kat. In the other window now, Nina and Randy were getting ready to fire. Two more shots, all hitting the beast but having no observable impact.

Seconds were ticking, charge, attack, avoid, shoot. The fight was going nowhere fast without being able to bring the creature down. The sun would be peeking the horizon soon.

How the hell were they going to get a medevac helicopter in here with this thing? Caden thought to himself.

The beast made one last vain attempt at attacking Caden, and then as quickly as this battle started, the creature left, barreling up the trail to the mine shaft opening and disappearing. Almost as if on cue, the first rays of the sun peeked at the jagged mountain horizon.

Caden and Mingo looked at each other, relieved but not really believing that it had left or that this fight had even taken place.

Randy called from the cabin window, "Is it gone?"

Mingo nodded, unsure. "Yes."

Soon the entire troop, Nina, and Kat were outside breathing a sigh of relief for the welcomed daylight and for the beast disappearing into the mountains.

*****

After the helicopter medical evacuation of Reggie Townsend and some of the scouts, Caden and Mingo sat waiting for the state police and search parties. Questions would need to be asked and answered, statements taken, and bodies recovered.

Nina sat down by Caden; she lifted his arm and put it around her and then kissed him on the check.

Kat was sitting next to Mingo and pondering on the events of the past few days, and then suddenly she blurted out, "No more Mr. Hotties for me!" to which the group all laughed.

With the now warming sun coming up, Caden felt ready to drift off into a nap. "You know, Mingo, we've had some pretty strange days, but I think this one is one of the strangest by far."

Mingo just nodded and replied with a brief "Yep!"

Chapter 39

ESCAPE

The creature had moved quickly up mine shaft #5, across the small opening at the top of the mountain, and then down into the other shaft. Descending downhill into the second shaft, it finally moved with less urgency. The sun was coming up with the rays of cleansing light that could bring its destruction. The beast had made it across the small exposed opening and escaped into the darkness of the other shaft. Down here in the depths of this mountain hollow, this Wendigo was safe.

It moved past the narrow cavern that split to the left and continued down the main shaft going right and past the bones and human skulls, even deeper until coming to what appeared to be a dead-end. The great beast heaved on one side, forcing an opening to slide through. It then pushed the rock wall closed.

With its belly full of human flesh, blood, and gore, it would be content—at least for a time. It could feel the slumber of sleep coming on now that its appetite was quenched and its consumption of evil was complete.

The beast moved in the comfort and darkness of its own lair now, its yellow eyes seeing easily in the gloom. It slumbered past the boxes filled with raw silver and gold that once belonged to Silver Jack Driscoll and his Cree Indian companion Edward Smith from days long gone. In a far dry corner was a nest of sorts made of branches and animal skins. This was where the great beast would lie and slumber until its next awakening.

On its last awakening, it had risen first as a blind old man, crippled, ancient, and weak. For its next awakening, it would crawl forth as a human resembling very much in appearance that of the man once known as Dirk Astor. Then, after once again coming into the scent of evil and blood, it would return to its terrible and formidable form of the Wendigo.

Chapter 40

LIFE

It had been three weeks now since the events up in the Huron Mountains. Caden, Mingo, Kat with her new boyfriend were busy at the outside grill drinking a beer, yacking it up, and laughing. The Upper Peninsula gray sky had started spitting snow, but the cover of the Catrin porch kept the snow and wind out. Inside the Catrin rustic log home in the kitchen, Susan Catrin, Nina Orend, Amanda Adams, and Claire Peterson were drinking wine, chatting, and preparing for an afternoon meal.

Down in the Catrins' basement family room, Sydney Willington was playing a game of doubles ping-pong with three scouts. Troy Jackson was sitting on a couch with three other scouts playing a video game called *Black Ops*. The remainder of the scouts were in an open area of the basement laughing as they were all wearing head-mounted white goggles. Individually, the boys were moving about yelling to each other, kicking and jabbing into empty air, playing a virtual reality game called *Space Pirate Trainer*.

Up in the huge Great Room, a fire was roaring in the fireplace. Sitting around the room with the news playing on the big-screen TV were Jake Catrin, FBI Agent John Anderson, and Adventure Bound Scout leaders Reggie Townsend and Randy Adams. The men were talking quietly, enjoying the comfort of fire and one another's company.

The Catrins had invited the group to their lodge for the weekend with the intent of providing some closure to the events a few weeks prior. The gathering was also intended as a reunion for the friends who had bonded after the Huron Mountain fiasco. To the Catrins' pleasant surprise, just about everyone was able to make it.

"Okay...here it is," said Jake's friend, John Anderson, pointing at the big screen.

Jake turned up the volume to hear the breaking news on the channel. On screen was a local Upper Peninsula station with a couple talking heads in the newsroom and two different on-the-site reporters.

The woman and the man from the Marquette newsroom location began by announcing a breaking story about a major drug, prostitution, and kidnapping ring being brought down with the cooperation of the FBI and local law enforcement.

The station then played a prerecorded press briefing from a conference room of the Marquette City Hall. There standing at the podium was Agent Anderson giving an overview of the interstate investigation of a criminal operation that was trafficking illegal drugs and prostitutes. The crime syndicate was based out of New York but was trafficking in Marquette, Michigan, and around the Great Lakes region. The recording then showed Anderson talking about how the investigation also uncovered the kidnapping of local victims mostly of college age. The recorded press briefing continued with Anderson thanking the state and local law enforcement for their support and then handed off the briefing to a local state police representative and then the mayor of Marquette. Finally, they opened up the conference to questions from the various press representatives. The press briefing cut off there and went to an on-site reporter standing in front of the Huron Mountain Club.

The attractive female reporter appeared to be positioned in front of the gate of the Huron Mountain Club. She described how investigations had revealed how local workers had made ties with the New York mob and were assisting in the human and drug trafficking. The whole operation took place without the knowledge of any members of the super elite and confidential list of the conservatory owners of the Huron Mountain Club. The reporter then went to describe a hero and member of the HMC, Dirk Astor, who was instrumental in uncovering the criminal enterprise and alerting local officials. The wide screen then flashed up a picture of a strikingly handsome college student—Dirk Astor. She went into some general descriptions of his heroic actions, how he had died heroically and how a memorial statue was going to be erected at Michigan Tech University in his honor. This was in addition to a generous endowment in his name and also a HMC endowment to Northern Michigan University. The woman then moved to another attractive woman, who was introduced as the public relations representative from the Huron Mountain club. This woman went on to thank the community for its outpouring of support and how the HMC remained committed to working with any further investigations and continuing their generous support to the community of Marquette and their continuing place as a leading conservancy for the environment in the Upper Peninsula of Michigan.

The news view on the TV screen then switched back to the talking heads in the newsroom who gushed over the great works and contributions of the Huron Mountain Club as they praised their efforts to fight crime in the Marquette area.

Kat had just walked in the room from out on the porch carrying a platter of grilled chicken, burgers, and hot dogs. "That's such bullshit!" she blurted out.

FBI Agent John Anderson turned and replied, "You are right, Kat. They edited and cut out the key points of the news conference. But guess who owns the local media stations? They are all subsidiaries, which are owned by Astor Enterprises."

Caden, Mingo, and Kat's new boyfriend, Ted, had just stepped in the door and heard the last part of the conversation, including Kat's outburst. Caden and Mingo looked at each other, then at Jake, then back to John Anderson, who shrugged his shoulders, as if to say there was nothing he could do about it.

Susan now stepped into the Great Room and announced, "Let's eat!" Then she looked at Caden, saying, "Can you please call everyone from the basement?"

The long rustic heavy wood table fit almost everyone. Kat, her boyfriend, and two scouts volunteered to sit at the folding table, which extended the length of the main table. Everyone had cycled through the food laid out at the kitchen bar, buffet style, had plates piled with food, and was sitting around the table.

"Let's pray," Susan announced.

With all heads bowed, Jake led a thanksgiving Christian blessing for the meal, friendship, and life. At the prayer conclusion, everyone finished with an "Amen."

Caden then raised his glass and toasted, "May the good guy with a gun always defeat the bad guy with the gun!"

To which Mingo replied with the second part of the toast, "And may good always defeat evil!"

"Hear, hear!" was the response from around the table.

With that, everyone started digging hungrily into their meals. The mood was happy, and everyone was chatting loudly while enjoying the new bonds of friendship forged in the wilds of Michigan's Upper Peninsula.

And thus ends this Yooper's tale.

About the Author

Robert Williams was born and raised in Michigan. He is retired and has resided in the Upper Peninsula after thirty years of travel and service to his country. He is an avid outdoorsman, survival expert, Second Ranger Battalion veteran, student of life, and now author. This book is dedicated to our service members, past and present, their families who have helped bear the weight and sacrifice of their service, and the communities that support them.